Where There's a Wil, There's a Way

PT Ambler

Where There's a Wil, There's a Way

A fledgling butler with a legacy to uphold.
A celebrity boss with a family to protect.
Crossing the upstairs/downstairs divide has never felt so
natural...nor so perilous.

...

This is the one, Wil thinks when he interviews for the butler
position at Buck House, Oxfordshire.

Dream home.

Dream job.

Dream boss...maybe.

...

Worst idea ever, Rhys thinks when he's convinced to employ a
butler straight out of the academy.

His privacy gone.

His sanity gone.

His heart...that might be gone, too.

Author's Note

A heart-felt thank you to my alpha, beta, and gamma reader brains trust – for seeing what I could no longer see, and for feeling the warm-fuzzy joy.

———— *ele* ————

To keep the story authentic to its English roots, the author has uses British English spelling and grammar.

Enjoy :)

Chapter 1

Wil

"What the hell do you think you're doing trying to be a butler? You're barely out of the cradle." The housekeeper's voice dripped disdain.

Wil clenched his fists tight. "I'm twenty—" The heavy teak door slammed in his face. "—two."

Shit.

"Worst day ever."

He resisted the urge to knock his forehead against the wood. The door didn't deserve such abuse. Then again, neither did he. In lieu of a stiff upper lip, Wil pasted on a fake smile, pulled his phone from his coat pocket, and pretend-scrolled through his oh-so-empty appointment calendar as though he had places to be, people to impress. He doubted it fooled anyone. Least of all his own psyche.

Twenty-seven interviews.

Twenty-seven times he'd rung the bell.

Twenty-seven times the door had opened, and he'd faced an expression that ranged from wonder to horror. More often on the horror end of that scale, truth be told.

Never mind starting his dream career. Down to one-hundred-and-eighty-six quid, and a quarter tank of fuel in his beat-up, hand-me-down, pea-green Ford Fiesta—if he didn't find a position soon, he'd have to crawl back home to Devon where his folks would fawn and fuss and suffocate every ounce of independence out of him.

Wil could practically hear his mother's voice.

Stay here in Devon, dear. You know how Lady Mistlethwaite is about keeping things in the family. She'd put you back on staff at the Manor in a jiffy. Your father isn't far off retirement. No more than five years. If you play your cards right, you could probably walk straight into his position.

Perhaps he should go back. Mistlethwaite Manor, and the bordering wilds of Exmoor, had always been his favourite part of the world to lick his wounds.

Heavy-footed, Wil wound his way back through Henley-upon-Thames' quaint streets, past shopfronts festooned with Halloween black and orange, retracing his steps to his rust-bucket car parked in the shadow of Henley's old town hall.

He dumped his leather folio, undid the button on his crisp blue suit jacket, collapsed his arse into the low bucket seat, and twisted his key in the ignition. "Please, please, please." The engine whined, then choked, then rumbled as it finally revved to life.

He twizzled the heater to high and sat back to wait for the insipid warmth to defrost the chill in his hands and his heart.

He would be okay. He had to be.

He had pedigree.

He had a shiny diploma from the prestigious Bourneworth Academy of Household Management.

The only other thing he needed was a foot in the door—for one brave soul to give him a chance.

Wil reversed as close as he could to the car parked behind him and clicked on his indicator, but before he could pull out into the mid-afternoon traffic, his phone's screen lit up with the Hardwick Household Services logo.

What did his agency want now? He slammed on the brake and swiped the screen. "Hello, this is Wil."

"Oh, thank goodness I caught you, Wil. It's Clara," she said, breathless. Which was odd. His contact at the agency usually had her shit together.

"Hello Clara. Are you okay?"

"Yes, yes. I'm fine, thank you dear. How was your interview?"

Did he have to say? It was like rubbing salt into the wound. "I suspect Mrs Satchwell will choose another applicant. A more mature applicant," Wil added. "Thank you for asking, though. I appreciated the opportunity." No sense in biting the proverbial hand that might, eventually, feed him.

"You're doing your best in a challenging industry." The woman was nothing if not diplomatic. "Don't lose heart."

Too late.

"Thanks for the pep talk, Clara. Did you need to speak to me about something?" He had places to be, angst to wallow in.

"Gosh, I'm so sorry, Wil. I called to see if you're still out near Henley. There's been an unfortunate snaffoo."

That didn't sound good. "A snaffoo?"

"Clerical error. Very unfortunate. We have you scheduled for another interview at the hour."

Wil's heart leaped, and he had to quell the urge to rip out into traffic. To move.

Think first, Wil. Then act.

"That's in fourteen minutes, Clara."

"Yes, I know. The gentleman was most particular about his availability. If you think you won't be able to get there in time, it might be better if we re-schedule."

"What's the address?" he asked. "I'm leaving Henley now."

"All I have is a property name, *Buck House*, and some rather cryptic directions. It's not one of my clients, so I can't offer much in the way of information, I'm afraid."

"I'm listening."

"It's a property near Hewstoke Woods. About five miles west of Henley. Look for Oak Tree Lane. At the end of the lane, you should see a black gate and a security cubby house...huh, that might be a typo. Who on earth would put their security in a cubby house?"

Wil plugged the address into his navigator app and a green squiggly line appeared. ETA thirteen minutes. He checked the time again. It'd be close. He flicked the indicator back on and pulled out as soon as the traffic cleared. "Who am I supposed to meet?"

"The client is a Mr Buckley. And the note here says to ask for Jacob. I'm so sorry for the last-minute notice. Rest assured, this will never happen again." Wil heard a hint of steel in Clara's voice.

Mister Jacob Buckley. No 'Sir' this or 'Lord' that. Just plain Jacob. It had a nice ring to it.

"Do you know anything about him?" Wil asked.

"Not much. The file is sparse, to say the least. You're the third and last to interview for the position."

One out of three. "Good odds."

"That it is. Would you like me to call ahead and inform them of the agency's error?"

Wil thought about it. Going in blind wasn't ideal, but all the preparation in the world hadn't got him a position yet. He had to try something new. "I think I might feel my way on this one. Wing it."

"Really? Better you than me. Call me if you have any difficulties."

"Thanks, Clara."

"Best of luck, Wil. I know you'll do brilliantly." With that vote of confidence, Clara hung up and left him alone to sink or swim.

Wil checked his watch. Two minutes had already gone the way of the dodo and he'd only just left the tight streets of Henley. Ahead of him, the country road broadened and inclined up into the beautiful beech woodlands of the Chilterns. He pressed his foot down, glorying in the light that gleamed gold through the autumn foliage.

"Twenty-eight," He reminded himself as he turned off the main road to the tiny hamlet of Cantnoor Cross, which wasn't much more than a crossroads with a church, a pub, and a shiny red post-box. Wil slowed as he steered down the narrow lane to Hewstoke Woods. On either side, the hedge groves grew high, leaning in over the lane like an evergreen hug. He plunged deep into the valley and over the clanking wooden bridge. Wil was so wrapped up in the beauty of the setting—in the light that streaked through the flaming canopy, and the thick carpet of amber leaves that covered the earth for the long slumber ahead—that he almost missed the turnoff to Oak Tree Lane. He swerved at the last second, his near-bald tyres spitting up mud and leaves as they sought traction.

True to Clara's word, the hooked lane ended at a black iron-work gate. On the right, nestled into the end of a dry-stone wall, was the promised cubby house. Only, it was more like a gothic Victorian era doll's house than a modern cubby house. Painted in shades of grey, with beady-eyed gargoyles set into the eaves, and a blood-red doorknob in the shape of a teardrop, the whole thing looked like something out of a ghoulish nightmare.

Wil cleared his expression of anything that might hint at 'young' and 'inexperienced' and 'risky', and pressed the tiny tear-shaped doorknob. Almost immediately, the central window on the upper story flickered to life, and a question popped up on the touchscreen.

What is the nature of your visit?

Below that were four optional answers:

1: Family

2: Business

3: Mischief

4: Lost

Wil was very tempted to choose option *3* to see what might happen, but he forced himself to tap *2: Business*. With any luck, it wasn't a trick question.

A *please wait* message drifted across the screen and Wil would swear the gargoyle in the upper right corner winked at him.

Just as the weirdness was feeling creepy enough for Wil to turn tail and run, the big, black gate swung open.

No going back now.

Pebbles sprang up under his wheels, popping against the undercarriage all the way to the house. By the time he got to the final turning circle, his nerves were popping along with them.

He shut off the engine and craned his head forward over his steering wheel to look up, amazed at the stone pile—Buck House—an exact scale replica of the gothic doll house at the gate, including the gargoyles in the eaves.

Door number twenty-eight.

Could this be the one?

The front door opened and a silver-haired, posture-perfect man emerged—the quintessential, distinguished butler. Wil couldn't believe the man's uncanny resemblance to his father. Surprisingly, it put him at ease.

"Good afternoon," he called as he climbed out of the car, squared his Windsor knot, re-buttoned his suit, and grabbed his folio from the passenger seat. Ready and raring for battle.

"William Haines?" Wil nodded. "I'm Jacob van der Shonn. Welcome to Buck House. Please come in."

Jacob *van der Shonn.* Not Buckley. That meant Mr Buckley was still an unknown quantity.

"Thank you." Wil stepped into the flagstone entry. "You're Mr Buckley's butler?"

"Me? A butler? Goodness, no." Jacob's perfectly aligned teeth flashed. "I'm Mr Buckley's assistant, researcher, book-keeper, and whatever else he throws at me."

"Oh. Interesting." And no help at all for Wil to figure out anything about Mr Buckley. He followed Jacob through the double entry and into a wide hall split in the middle by a grand floating staircase.

Murmuring voices came from above, and a grandfather clock beside the entry ticked the seconds by, but the house was oth-erwise still and serene. "It's a lovely home," Wil said, then he looked up to the second-floor landing and saw the head of a furry animal hanging on the wall. *Ugh.* His step stuttered. He'd never understood people who appreciated taxidermy. Then he realised it wasn't an animal at all. It was the decapitated head of a teddy bear.

"Are you okay?" Jacob asked.

Wil pointed up. "Poor teddy."

"Ah, Ted-head, the house mascot. He met an unfortunate end after we left him in the attic and mice used his body for a nest. Now he watches over all of us."

"Protection from mice?"

"Amongst other rodents." Jacob chuckled. "Let's head to my office to have a little chat, then you can meet Mr Buckley. Sound good?"

"Sounds wonderful."

He followed Jacob around the grand staircase to the back of the hall, catching quick glances through the open doors of two drawing rooms in the front, a large dining room on the left, and a darker room on the right. The space invited further inspection, but Jacob led him quickly through the ground floor, around to the shadowy underside of the stairs, and through a recessed door in the far-left corner of the hall.

"The kitchen is the real hub of the house," Jacob said.

"I can see why."

The enormous room had a glorious, warm feel. And not just because of the toasty heat emanating from the red enamel Aga cooking range. Hardwood bench tops ran in an L-shape along the wall between the Aga and a giant porcelain farm sink. Above the sink, a row of window boxes housed terracotta pots of thyme and rosemary and oregano that caught the afternoon light and filled the room with their living fragrance. In the centre of the space, gleaming copper pans hung over a huge, age-scarred wooden island encircled by simple bar stools.

"The whole back half of the ground floor is for domestic staff." Jacob pointed to four other doors along the same side of the room where they'd entered. "An office, pantry, laundry, and the last door leads to an old servants' stairwell. It goes up to the kid's rooms."

Kids? "Mr Buckley has children?"

"Oh, ah, yes, but not exactly." With that cryptic answer, Jacob waved him through the door to the office.

Compared to the rest of the house, the room was sterile. Its crisp-white walls, modern white desk, and pale-grey sofa cried out for colour.

"Take a seat, William."

"Thank you. Please call me Wil." He perched on one end of the sofa and put on his game face. If he lost the job, it wouldn't be through inattention.

"Sure." Jacob pulled out a hard-bound notebook and sat down at the other end. "Tell me about your butlering experience, Wil."

Should he point out that *butlering* wasn't actually a word? Meticulousness was a virtue for a butler, but it wasn't always an attractive trait.

"Strictly speaking, I've never actually been a butler, but my great-grandparents, grandparents, and my parents after them have served as the housekeeper and butler for a large estate in North Devon."

Jacob scanned his resume. "Mistlethwaite Manor?"

"Yes. I grew up there. Prior to attending the Bourneworth Academy of Household Management, I worked as Lord Mistlethwaite's valet."

"A unique upbringing."

"To some. But it was normal for me. Between the Manor and the Academy, my experiences have given me a solid grasp of traditional service, as well as fresh notions about how to manage a complex modern home." Did he sound too pompous? Just pompous enough? People with money had weird notions of how the help should behave. Lord Mistlethwaite was a traditionalist to the core. But not everybody expected bowing and scraping. Not in the twenty-first century.

"'A complex modern home'." Jacob repeated Wil's words. "Do you ever feel like you've regressed back to the nineteenth century?"

Wil nodded. "Frequently."

Jacob steepled his fingers, doing nothing to cover his quirk of a smile. "I like you, Wil Haines…"

That was a first.

"...and I'm very glad I convinced Mr Buckley to give the idea of getting a butler a go."

Wait. What? "Mr Buckley's never had a butler?"

"Exactly," Jacob nodded, which still left Wil in the dark about the identity of his prospective employer.

Dammit, Clara.

"Buck House is as much his place of work as it is his home. The housekeeper, Evangeline, who's been here so long she's practically part of the family, is going on personal leave soon. And I'm also stepping away from most of my domestic responsibilities by Christmas. Without us, he's going to need help running the house. Which reminds me, the successful applicant will need to sign a confidentiality agreement and abide by certain privacy measures, as I'm sure you understand, given Mr Buckley's position."

Wil understood nothing, but he nodded anyway. "A wise move," he said, hoping the response was vaguely appropriate. If he wasn't careful, he risked being tripped up by his own ignorance.

Who was Mr Buckley?

The minute Wil was alone, he'd pull out his phone to do comprehensive research on the man. No stone left un-turned. "Are there any other staff?" he asked.

"No, just me and Evangeline, with casual help that comes in whenever we host a dinner party or other event. That's all we've needed. Up till now."

"Why not employ a temporary housekeeper?" Wil asked. "I don't want to talk myself out of a position, but with so few staff in a relatively small house, employing a butler seems unwarranted. What am I missing?"

"Mr Buckley would never do anything to make Evangeline feel like she's being replaced."

Loyalty. Wil liked it. "You mentioned children, but not a Mrs Buckley." Wil unashamedly fished.

"Oh, gosh, no." Jacob laughed. "There's a *Ms* Buckley, Mr Buckley's sister, but she's rarely here."

A single father. With multiple children.

Wil was starting to worry. What if the kids were spoiled brats? He was a butler, not a manny. He wasn't equipped to spend his days wiping noses and tidying away toys. "Will I meet Mr Buckley today? And the children?"

"Possibly," Jacob's voice cooled. "Just a few more questions."

"Please," he encouraged. The more clues to Mr Buckley's identity, the better.

"What's your opinion of Mr Buckley's reputation?"

That stumped him. How could he have an opinion? He didn't even know who the man was?

Time for some diplomatic fudge. "I hardly think it matters what my opinion is of his reputation, professional or otherwise. If I have one, it's not my place to voice it."

Jacob pursed his lips and made a notation in his notebook. "How would you characterise the way you relate to children?"

That was simple. "Depends on the child. They're as individual as any adult."

"If you could choose any three people to invite to your dream dinner party, who would you invite?"

Really? If he had to answer that question one more time, he would scream.

Wing it, Wil. This is your chance to stand out from the crowd.

"Do they have to be real people?" he asked.

"No. Choose whoever you like."

Wil thought for a second. "MC Escher, Michaelangelo, and Aragorn."

"Interesting. Two artists and a fictional character."

"I like creatives."

"I guess you do. Why Escher?" he asked.

"I get lost in his work."

"Hmm. I'll excuse you the pun."

"Thank you."

"And Michaelangelo. Why him?"

"Dedication to his craft. The man was a master."

"And Aragorn?"

"Son of Arathorn," Wil clarified, then immediately wished he could take it back. Had he read the whole situation wrong? Was Jacob serious with his paint-by-numbers question?

"Not Gandalf?" Jacob asked?

Oh, thank God. "No." At Jacob's raised brow, Wil figured he might as well go for broke. "Aragorn is much easier on the eye."

Jacob laughed as he snapped his notebook shut. "Promise you'll send me an invitation to your dream dinner party?"

Wil expelled all the air in his lungs. He hadn't screwed himself over after all. "Deal."

"Are you open to fixed dates for your annual holiday leave?"

Wil sat up straighter than straight. This was getting real. "It depends when the fixed dates would be, but I'm open to discussion."

"The hours are generally nine-to-five while here at Buck House, except for the nights Mr Buckley hosts his dinner parties, and such. When he's travelling, the hours would flex and extend as needed. To offset the extra hours, Mr Buckley has included eight weeks of annual leave into the permanent contract. Four of those weeks will be fixed in the summer when the children are home from school. The timing for the remaining four weeks is up for negotiation."

Eight weeks? Wow. "That's generous." Not that he'd have argued if it was less. He wasn't looking for the dream anymore. A job was a job. The prospect of a steady pay cheque was more than enough...for the moment.

Jacob nodded. "Do you have an up-to-date British passport?"

"Yes." Did it matter that he'd never actually used it?

"Excellent. Shall we take the rest of the tour then, Mr Haines?"

His breath left his lungs in a great rush. Getting through the front door had been the first hurdle. Getting through the interview made Wil feel like a champion. "Absolutely, Mr van der Shonn. Lead the way."

Under Ted-head's beady gaze, they took the main stairs to the rectangular gallery around which were six closed doors, evenly dispersed. It would have been dark if it wasn't for the dandelion chandelier that hung from the high ceiling into the open space created by the floating stair. "This second floor is for family. Mr Buckley, the children, and Miriam, plus a suite for guests."

"Miriam?"

"Mr Buckley's sister." Jacob gave him an odd side-eye, then went on. "The door behind you leads up to the attic. If the new butler chooses to live in, that's where they'll reside." Jacob shot him a glance. "Would you like to take a look?"

Would he ever. "Absolutely. Thank you."

"After you. Mind your head at the top."

Clearing the beam at the top of the narrow, switch-back stairs, Wil looked up to find an amazing space. The white panelled walls made it feel light and airy, despite the steep angle of the pitched roof. At one end was a screened bathroom, complete with a roll-top, claw-footed tub, and next to that was a simple but functional kitchenette. The true wonder of the studio, though, was the combination bedroom and sitting room at the far end, where French doors opened onto a Juliette balcony nestled up close to a giant oak tree. "Wow."

"Do you like it?"

Like was putting it mildly. "It's stunning." And to think that it could be his. A place to make his—a home, a career, a life. Buck House was nothing like Mistlethwaite Manor. It wasn't a grand estate. It didn't come with a title, livery, and a coat of arms. It wasn't anything like what he'd been looking for. And yet, it felt better than anything he could have imagined.

There had to be a catch.

Wil opened the French doors and stepped out onto the tiny balcony. He didn't even need to reach to touch one of the many amber leaves that rustled paper-light in the chilly breeze. "It's like being in a treehouse." He looked back over his shoulder in time to catch a thoughtful expression cross Jacob's face.

"Hmm." Hands in his pockets, Jacob rocket back onto the heels of his shoes. "Ready to meet the boss?" he asked.

Finally! "That's a trick question, right?"

Out came a genuine smile.

From the second-floor landing, Jacob headed to one of the doors on the side of the gallery. Muffled giggles met his brisk knock. "Mr Buckley?"

"Enter," came a high-pitched voice, followed by more giggles, and Jacob turned the knob and pushed open the door.

Wil held back in the doorway, conscious that the room was a private space. From his vantage, all he could see was the end of a bed, piled high with a gaudy rainbow of dresses—old-fashioned ball gowns with voluminous skirts.

This was a child's room?

"Why is Jacob calling you Mr Buckley?" someone out of view asked. It sounded like a girl.

"No idea, Lex. Shall we ask him?" Came another voice. A high, syrupy falsetto that did not sound at all like a girl. "Jacob, why are you calling me Mr Buckley? Can't you see I'm a lady?"

Mouth pursed with contained laughter, Jacob swung the door wider, revealing two ladies—if Wil could call them that—one older, one younger, preening in front of a full-length mirror. Their red and purple gowns were magnificent, but their wigs were matted, their teeth were black with rot, and their makeup was caked and smeared. They looked more at home in a brothel than a ballroom. Added to that, the older 'lady', who was coming toward Wil, had a thick beard that bristled through her makeup.

Was this the elusive Mr Buckley? The man who could become his boss?

What to do? Pretend like everything was normal? Pretend like *anything* at Buck House had been normal?

Was it a test?

Wing it, Wil.

"My Lady Buckley." Wil did his best to keep a straight face as he reached for her proffered fingers, bowed, and pressed a gentlemanly kiss to the scattering of black hairs on the back of her hand. "A pleasure to meet you."

"And you, Mr Haines." Still in character, she curtsied, pulled her fingers from his loose grip, and twirled back to the mirror where she and the younger lady collapsed in a fit of giggles.

Jacob shook his head. "Don't mind them, Wil. Come on. I'll show you the grounds."

Had he gone too far?

Had he lost his chance?

Unsure what to do, Wil turned to follow Jacob, but on the edge of his vision he noticed the older lady's eyes reflected in the mirror follow him as he walked out the door, crinkled with amusement and...something more.

Chapter 2

Rhys

The flickering flames of the open fire and the finger of scotch in his hand would send most people to sleep. For him, though, it was like a shot of caffeine. He was a pro at harnessing the energy of the night—his Petri dish of inspiration—a time when his ideas germinated and grew to life. Most of his nights felt like a tornado of creativity, and he eagerly rode the whirligig to other worlds. But that night, Jacob had cornered him for another purpose entirely.

Rhys clicked play on the sound-system remote, and a rich melody played by a solo viola swirled around them.

"Nice," Jacob said. "Is this from the *Barrow* soundtrack?"

"Yeah. Delicious melody, isn't it?"

"Mournful."

Rhys nodded at Jacob's apt description. "Hector and I argued over the viola, but it's the perfect instrument."

"Hector knows his stuff."

"Yeah."

"Talking about good HR choices...what's your take on our interviewees from today?"

Rhys groaned. He didn't cotton to new people too easily, let alone having a stranger live in his house. "Do I have to?" It was Jacob's fault that Buck House needed a butler in the first place—deserting Rhys in his time of need. Although, in Rhys' opinion, *need* was far too strong a word. He'd do just fine rattling around on his own. "I could just employ one of those virtual assistants. They can do most of the organising. I don't need anyone here."

Jacob's silence was answer enough as he pushed the three slim files across the small table between their winged-back chairs.

Rhys tried another tack. "I just don't get this butler thing. Why would anyone ever want to be 'in service'? Master of somebody else's domain? It's alien to me. Why would anyone want to live someone else's life, and not their own?"

"Everyone's unique, with individual career aspirations."

"True."

"If everyone dreamed of making films, you'd have stiffer competition."

"Also, true." His waking dreams might never be brought to the big screen.

"It might surprise you to know that most butlers have personalities pretty damn close to your control-freakish ways."

Rhys frowned. That was pushing it.

Jacob tightened the screw. "After all, it takes a lot of self-assurance and initiative to take charge of someone else's house."

"I'm not a control freak."

"Does the phrase *creative control* not ring a bell?"

"That's different. That's work."

Jacob interlocked his fingers. "That's your work. This is their work. There is no discernible difference."

Rhys grunted, not at all convinced. Having control and being a freak about it were two different things. "I feel like they'd be living my life vicariously. It's weird."

"Weird, huh? Don't you live your character's lives vicariously?"

"That's different."

"Mmm-hmm." Jacob's expression said it all. "Who's your first choice?"

Not ready to give in, Rhys flicked through the three files while Jacob's silence grew. "Who do you think?" he asked, throwing the decision back into Jacob's court.

"I'm here to get your honest opinion, not to reinforce my own. What did you think of Mrs Robard?"

"She's, ah... is there a polite synonym for irritating?" Jacob might accuse him of being a control freak, but that woman wore the word persnickety like a crown.

"That's a no, then," Jacob said, knowing him well enough to not even ask the question. "And Mr Smithson?"

Rhys tapped the cover of the second file with a finger. "He has some serious gravitas. Heavy on the serious."

"He'd make a superb butler. All the neighbours would be jealous as hell to know you have him at your beck and call."

Rhys waved that notion off. He cared about his neighbours' jealousy even less than he did about having someone at his beck and call. "He uses antiquated words like *chap*. Who does that anymore? Besides, he's way too stick-in-the-mud to deal with

Lex and Syd." Rhys was amazed Jacob hadn't automatically ruled him out.

Rhys dropped Mr Smithson's dossier on top of Mrs Robard's, then picked up the third option. "Mr Haines. He's young." Attractive, too, but Rhys wasn't about to broadcast that thought.

Jacob's lips twitched. "If we're going for jealousy, he'd be even more of a prize."

"To some."

"To anyone with eyes." Jacob's twitch turned into a knowing grin.

"Oh, for fucks sake, Jacob. It's bad enough that I have to let a stranger invade my home, now you think I should welcome him into my bed, too? Hell no."

At that wildly dramatic leap, Jacob's eyebrows went up.

Rhys sighed into his scotch, the heat of his breath making the glass cloud up, then clear. "Sorry. It's just..."

"You don't trust easily. I know."

Not where his home was concerned. Why should he? But Rhys hadn't got where he was in life without being courageous. He flicked open the file and scanned the details. "What's your gut tell you?"

"He notices things."

"Things?"

"He noticed your Ted on the wall."

"Ted-head is a gem."

"You would say that. Wil looked a little sad at the sight of him."

"Interesting."

"Most people think it's macabre to mount a teddy bear's head like it was a red deer stag, hunted in its prime."

"Most people should think it macabre to mount a deer's head. Unlike a deer, the teddy bear was never actually alive. You can assure any who ask, Ted did not suffer on his path to greatness."

Jacob chuckled. "I can just see it in the credits of one of your films. 'No teddy bears were hurt in the making of this movie'."

Rhys snorted. Trust Jacob. "That would put a lot of children's minds at rest."

A comfortable silence stretched out between them. Eventually, though, Jacob stirred. "He is young. Neither tried nor tested."

"And yet..." Rhys' pulse kicked up a pace.

Jacob nodded sagely. "And yet..."

The glow of fire-light licked through Rhys' glass as he lifted it in a silent toast of assent. As much as he wanted to, Rhys couldn't bring himself to say no. "A one-month trial. No longer."

"I'll call Hardwick Household Services tomorrow," Jacob said. "When do you want him to start?"

"Monday." Rhys had never been one to put off the inevitable. "The sooner he starts, the sooner the trial ends."

"Indeed." Jacob threw back the last of his scotch, collected the files into his briefcase, and left Rhys to his musings.

Chapter 3

Wil

S tep one—get the job.

Step two—don't screw up.

"Head high, Wil. You can do this." From his unpacked suitcases, Wil grabbed his document folio, and a notebook and pen, and made his way down from his attic rooms to the kitchen where Jacob had promised a steaming cup of tea.

The space was as huge and as glorious as Wil remembered. The mid-morning sun streamed through the south-facing windows and bounced warm off of the copper pans. It assuaged his first-day nerves.

"English Breakfast, Lady Grey, Earl Grey, green tea, rosehip and hibiscus, or peppermint?" Jacob asked.

"Someone likes the Greys."

"Mm-hmm. Rhys is very particular about his hot beverages. My best tip for you is to never get between the man and his mug."

"Noted. Earl Grey, please."

"Good choice." Jacob flicked the lid on one of the ceramic cannisters beside the window ledge and loaded a tea basket with loose leaves. "One day you should see him make hot chocolate. Just be warned, don't try it if you're tee-totalling. The adult version packs a whammy."

"Do you call him Rhys or Mr Buckley?"

"Rhys. We're not all that formal around here. That was just for your benefit."

Calling the place informal was an understatement. Buck House was like night and day to Mistlethwaite Manor.

"So...I did some more research on Buck House over the weekend."

"*More* research?" Jacob flashed Wil an amused look over the wire rim of his glasses. "You've discovered who Mr Buckley is, haven't you?"

"Ahh..." *Shit*. "Was it that obvious?" Wil winced. Mortified. The minute he'd heard the name Buckley, he ought to have recognised Rhys as the darling of the British film industry.

"Blatantly." Jacob chuckled. "Don't worry about it, though. When I spoke to Clara at the agency, she told me they gave you almost no time to prepare."

Wil took a stalling sip of tea. "I didn't like to say."

"Don't worry about it. Future reference, though, we value truth over politeness in this house. And I'm sorry I found some amusement at your expense."

Wil waved the apology away. "A fresh start?"

"Sounds good," Jacob said. "How's your tea?"

"Perfect, thank you."

"Excellent. Let's get to the particulars, then."

Jacob opened a manila file on the table. Inside was a short stack of papers with at least a dozen sticky notes attached.

It looked so official. And the reality of the moment slammed into Wil.

Rhys Buckley's butler.

This is your chance, Wil. Do not screw it up.

"Before we get into the nitty-gritty, let's start with the confidentiality agreement."

"Of course."

"As you can see, it's a standard agreement disallowing release of any information about Mr Buckley's private life or of his company, Buckle Up Productions, unless you're given express permission, or it's required for legal purposes."

"I'll be involved in Buckle Up Productions, too?" That was a surprise.

"Mr Buckley *is* Buckle Up Productions. It's best to assume that every piece of information you come across during your employment is privileged. Once you've signed this agreement, it is in effect for perpetuity whether you have a position here at Buck House or not. If you agree, please sign here."

It grated to think such a thing was necessary, but Wil knew it was standard operating procedure. Particularly for people of interest to the tabloids.

Wil uncapped his favourite fountain pen and signed.

"Excellent. Now, let's turn our attention to the full employment contract."

"Are you a lawyer?" He sounded like one.

Jacob laughed. "Almost. This semester I'll graduate with my Juris Doctor."

"Wow. That's impressive." Especially given the guy was old enough to be his father. "Guess it's never too late to make a career move." He'd never wanted to be anything other than a butler.

Jacob gave a gracious nod in thanks.

"Doesn't matter how many degrees you get, old man," came a deep voice from the doorway. "I'll still decimate you at Scrabble."

Startled, Wil spun around.

"Ah, the prodigal child," said Jacob.

"Ah, the mighty mage," Mr Buckley jabbed back.

Wil stared. Stunned.

In well-worn black jeans and a soft charcoal knit sweater, Rhys Buckley looked nothing like the harlot in face paint he'd met at his interview. In fact, he didn't look much like the slick director photographed in the most recent *Film Quarterly* either. His finger-combed black hair hung in messy waves, and a jaw full of thick bristles against chalk-pale skin enhanced the hollows of his cheeks. He looked like something out of a vampire novel—dangerous and sexy as hell.

It was impossible for Wil not to track Rhys as he crossed the kitchen to the retro chrome espresso machine where, with practiced movements, Rhys fired up the bean grinder, packed and tamped the portafilter, and brewed a demitasse of espresso.

Wil couldn't have looked away if he'd tried.

"Wil?"

Tiny cup in hand, Rhys turned and leaned back against the bench top, ankles crossed. His thick, dark eyelashes fluttered shut as he inhaled the brew's aroma.

"Wil?"

God. Never before had Wil wanted to *be* a beverage.

Drink me down.

"William!"

"Huh?" Wil jerked in surprise.

Arms crossed, eyebrows raised—Jacob was either pissed or amused.

Shit. Both were bad news.

"Ready, Mr Haines?"

"Yes, yes. I'm...sorry. I'm with you." *Sort of.*

While Jacob slid another copy of Wil's trial contract Mr Buckley's way, Wil took a steadying gulp of tea and tried to focus, but the words swam on the page.

"This contract will serve for the stipulated one-month trial period, and provides a foundation for the ongoing contract."

"If I pass the trial."

"Exactly. You might have noticed that there are a few sections which allow for negotiation. I've filled in Rhys' specific requests, but there is space for any necessary additions you both agree to today. I suggested to Mr Buckley..."

"Rhys," Rhys said.

"My apologies...to Rhys, that even though most of these arrangements won't come into effect until after the trial period concludes, it would be best to discuss them now to ensure expectations are in accord."

"There you go with the big words again," Rhys teased.

Jacob seemed to ignore him. "As I'm sure you can imagine, Rhys' schedule is variable. On average, he spends a third of the year on location, where we set up a base of operations. I think of it as his home away from home. Where he goes, you will go."

"So, it's not so much Buck House that needs a butler as Mr Buckley himself?" Wil ventured.

"Exactly. The line between the butler and personal assistant roles will blur. His affairs are quite complicated, as you might imagine."

"For example?" A montage of Rhys Buckley's potential 'affairs' flashed through Wil's mind, and he could feel the heat rise to his cheeks. Thank God Jacob had given him a large mug of tea to hide behind.

Yep, that's me—thirsty as a camel.

"Nothing too onerous. General organisation and care for his temporary residence, usually hosting in-house, plus the occasional off-site meeting that might require catering and such. He has a driver, but you'll need to organise other ad hoc travel and accommodation. There's no real routine, so Rhys will have to give you specifics of what he needs in that respect as it presents itself. On location, he works eighteen-plus-hour days and he'll basically need you to run his life while he's living it." He looked over at Rhys. "Is that a fair assessment?"

"Let's just say my DP would be shocked if my socks ever matched."

"DP?" Wil asked.

"Director of Photography."

"I guess matching socks are a low priority, relatively speaking," said Wil.

"You could say that. But then I've never had a butler at my beck and call before, so things could be looking up for my sock drawer."

They all looked down at Rhys' feet. He was wearing two perfectly matching, warm and snuggly red woollen socks. At a couple of inches over six feet, Rhys was a rangy man. There was nothing snuggly about him. But Wil wanted to hug his feet. Which was all kinds of weird. It was a disturbing way to discover a possible foot fetish. Or maybe it was just a Rhys Buckley fetish.

Wil felt his cheeks flame as hot as the socks.

"Questions?" Jacob asked him.

"No." Absolutely none.

"Well, then..." Jacob cast Rhys an enquiring look. At Rhys' nod, he said, "The trial's yours, if you want it."

If he wanted it? Of course, he bloody well wanted it.

Money in the bank.

Time to prove himself worthy.

A home to make his own...well, an attic to make his own, and the rest of Buck House to manage as he saw fit, while working up close and very personal with *the* Rhys Buckley.

Screw decorum. It took effort not to blot the page with ink in his haste to sign his name.

"Welcome aboard, Wil."

"Thank you, Jacob. And thank you, Mr Buckley. I appreciate the opportunity."

"My name is Rhys. This *Mr Buckley* business is weirding me out."

Jacob chuckled. "You sound like Lex."

Lex? Wil catalogued the name for future reference.

"Channelling a thirteen-year-old is easy," Mr Buckley replied, then turned to Wil. "Seriously, call me Rhys. Everyone does."

Calling him by his given name felt like crossing a line—an uncomfortable step toward intimacy. Which was ridiculous. It was the twenty-first century. They might be boss and butler, but he didn't have to call Rhys lord and master.

Wil nodded. "As you wish."

Rhys tipped back his head and sang, "As you wish!" He elbowed Jacob. "Love a man who knows his way around *The Princess Bride*."

"You know *The Princess Bride*?" He'd never met another guy who knew it. Besides David, of course. But they'd grown up in each other's pockets, and since one of David's nannies liked to play DVDs of old movies during nap time, Wil couldn't have avoided the movie if he'd tried.

"Of course. Total classic. Can I call you Wil?"

"Oh. Ah. Sure. I mean, yes, of course. Call me Wil."

A click of the door, a rush of damp, cold air, and the arrival of a very pregnant woman interrupted his word vomit. Thank God.

Wil was on his feet, prepared to help, but Rhys was already there.

"Angel! You're a sight for sore eyes."

"Why thank you, good sir." She eyed Wil. "And who might this be? Goodness, Rhys. Did you go out clubbing and find a keeper?"

A keeper?

"Behave, Evangeline," Jacob admonished.

"Why?"

"Come meet Wil. He's our new butler," explained Jacob.

"Butler?" Her eyes skittered around the kitchen, looking for a hidden camera. "Is this a joke? Are you pranking me right now?"

"No joke." Jacob said.

"I wish." Rhys muttered at the same time.

Evangeline frowned. She leaned back against the now-shut door and shared a long look with Rhys. "You're serious."

"Mm-hmm."

"But, he's so young." She switched her attention to Wil, staring at him as though he was an animal at the zoo.

Rhys chuckled. "You'd make an outstanding detective, Angel."

"Huh. I always thought butlers were old and, like, uptight."

"Not always." If Wil had a quid for every time he'd had to correct that assumption, he'd be rich enough to employ his own butler.

"Fair enough. I'm Evangeline. Housekeeper extraordinaire," she challenged.

Wil rounded the bench and offered his hand. "Wil Haines, butler *par excellence*."

She cracked a smile. "Ha! I like that." That detente resolved, Evangeline shrugged off her coat and scarf. "What's for breakfast then, boss?"

Breakfast? Wil checked his watch. It was nearer lunch time.

"Mmm." Rhys rubbed his hands together. "Pancakes, bacon, and lashings of syrup, thanks Angel."

"Sweet tooth," Evangeline teased.

Rhys shrugged. "The kids go back to school tonight. We all deserve one last treat before the real world comes crashing in."

"Works for me." Evangeline lifted two of the lids on the Aga hob and placed large skillets on each to heat. Once she had bacon crisping, she whisked buttermilk, eggs, and flour and ladled out four perfect rounds of pancake batter.

Meanwhile, Rhys and Jacob moved in well-practiced accord, setting places for five, and gathering maple syrup, chocolate nubs, and three kinds of fruit preserves into the middle of the kitchen island.

"Can I help?" Wil asked.

"No need." Jacob clapped him on the shoulder as he passed. "Drink your tea. Enjoy the calm before the storm."

"That sounds ominous."

"Shush, Jacob." Evangeline admonished as she flipped the golden pancakes onto a growing stack and ladled another set. "You'll scare the boy."

Wil contented himself listening to them chatter. The better he understood the personal dynamics of the household, the better he could do his job. It amazed him at how informal they were with each other. It was especially odd to see Rhys muck in. In Wil's experience, people who had domestic help rarely lifted a finger.

Having said that, he'd grown up in Lord and Lady Mistlethwaite's household, whose various titles could readily be used by the *Oxford English Dictionary* as examples of the word 'crusty'. That was his normal. Buck house was...not.

He never would've dreamed of becoming friends with his employer the way Evangeline and Jacob clearly were with Rhys. They made it seem so natural.

Wil eyed Rhys. How would it feel to be friends with his boss?

His stomach squirmed again, and it wasn't with hunger.

It wasn't until he noticed three sets of eyes on him that Wil realised someone had asked him a question. "Sorry. The aroma of bacon swept me away."

Evangeline flashed him a smile. "Bacon has that effect on Rhys, too."

"Does not."

"Does too."

"Children." Jacob sighed. "Ask your question, Evangeline."

"I asked where's the best place to go butlering...be a butler...whatever the word is." She waved her greasy spatula in the air, searching. "You know what I mean."

"In Britain, or the world?"

"Britain, either, both."

"I can think of a few hubs where the rich and famous play." Jacob listed them on his fingers. "London, Paris, Milan..."

"Dubai, Tokyo, Singapore, New York..." Rhys weighed in.

"Depends if you're looking for wealth, culture, or tradition. There are some incredibly opulent homes in the Middle East where no expense is spared. East Asia too. Buckingham Palace is the peak in Britain. The most prestigious. The butlers who've served there are famous. And the term is butling."

That bit of trivia seemed to stump them all, till Rhys broke the silence. "Would you add butling to the Buck House dictionary, Jacob? For the next time we play scrabble."

They all chuckled, and Wil sighed with relief. "Buck House comes pretty close, though. For butling, I mean."

"Oh, no doubt about that," Rhys said. "Buck House is a one of a kind."

"Agreed," said Jacob.

Thudding feet down the back stairway heralded a young boy, who Wil guessed was about seven or eight years old. He tore into the kitchen and ran straight to Evangeline.

"Whoa, slow down, Munchkin."

"Is breakfast ready yet?"

"Almost." The batter sizzled as she poured another four ladles full onto the griddle.

"Pancakes?" the boy asked with a gap-toothed grin.

"Yep," said Evangeline. "And bacon."

"Yum." He plonked a metal thing that looked like a mangled insect with wires and hinges and springs going in every direction on the island table top, then climbed up onto his stool.

The boy was a Buckley, no doubt. His green eyes and high cheekbones were identical to Rhys', and his hair was the same mess of shoulder-length tar-black curls.

"Please excuse Syd, Wil. He has no manners." When Rhys had the boy's attention, he said, "Syd, this is Wil. He's going to be living and working here for a bit."

Wil stiffened at the 'for a bit' comment, not needing any reminders that he was on trial.

"Look sharp munchkin, hot stuff coming through." Evangeline set a ceramic platter of crispy bacon and a generous stack of pancakes down in the middle of the island. The Buckley family sure didn't do things by halves.

"Rhys, can you please call Lex down?" Evangeline asked.

"Sure, Angel." Rhys sent off a quick text message.

"You'll get fat letting your phone do the walking," Evangeline admonished her boss.

Rhys looked at the steaming stack of pancakes and shook his head. "I don't think it's the phone that'll make me fat, Angel."

Barely a minute later, Wil heard another clatter of footsteps, and a teenaged girl arrived. She too shared Rhys' high cheekbones, but her black hair hung dead straight to her waist.

"And this is Lex. Say hi, Lex."

"Hi."

Wil did a double take when he realised that the girl, Lex, was the other Halloween harlot.

The transformation was incredible.

Lex slid onto the stool beside Wil and arranged one pancake, one rasher of bacon, and one tiny dollop of maple syrup on her plate.

"And that's everyone." Rhys made jazz hands at the group before also tucking in.

Still no mention of a mother.

Was Rhys divorced?

Widowed?

Wil's Google search mentioned nothing about Rhys having children. In fact, Wil hadn't been able to find much private information at all.

He was a puzzle.

No way were the kids adopted. One look proved they shared Rhys' DNA.

Not that the nuclear family was the only way to go. The children could be his by surrogacy. Rhys was more than wealthy enough to make that happen. And hadn't Evangeline teased him about going clubbing? Inferring that Rhys could've brought Wil home to Buck House for a shag. Which meant Rhys could be bi. Or gay. And available...

Not that Wil would ever make a move on his boss. Even if he was hot as hell.

"Wil?"

He jerked, surprised by Evangeline's hand on his shoulder. "What? Sorry."

"Aren't you hungry?"

"Oh, ah...yes." *In more ways than one.* "Sorry."

"No need to apologise, but help yourself to some breakfast before it's all gone. I swear this lot have metabolisms so fast they burn fire-engine red."

Wil couldn't help but laugh. Good to know he wasn't the only one burning red hot. "Thanks for the warning," he said, and reached for the tongs.

"Can we go shopping on the way back to school today, Uncle Rhys?" Lex asked.

Uncle Rhys?

Lex was his niece?

Oops.

That'll teach you not to make assumptions, Wil.

Relief warred with new nerves. Which was ridiculous. What did it matter if his boss was a father, or fancy free? It wasn't like Wil had any design on the man. He had a job to do. He would not let a little thing like attraction impede his performance.

Chapter 4

Rhys

"Can I help?" Wil hovered nearby, watching as Rhys helped Syd load his bags into the back of his swanky new Range Rover.

Black, of course, with charcoal leather seats.

Rhys dangled his car fob in a pincer grip for Wil to take. "You could start the engine and get the heater going."

"I can do that." Wil disappeared around the car with a crunch of pebbles underfoot, and Rhys turned his attention to Syd.

"Got your books? Football kit? Art folio?"

"Uh-huh."

"Are you sure? If I find any art or invention designs lying around the place, they will go into the fire."

Syd's eyes bulged with horror and he hurriedly burrowed back into his school bags.

Rhys wouldn't destroy anything his nephew made, but Syd was notorious at leaving a trail of unfinished creations, like inventor's breadcrumbs, in his wake.

"What about you, Lex?"

"What about me?"

"Am I going to find school things everywhere in your room?"

"No, because you don't go into my room when I'm not here." She flicked her long ponytail. "Privacy, Uncle Rhys. Remember?"

He ignored that. "What about your swim gear?"

"Got it."

"Hockey stick?"

"Yes." She rolled her eyes.

"Fabulous. Let's blow this popsicle stand."

"Uncle Rhys." Lex groaned.

"Soooo embarrassing." Rhys affected his niece's tone, and Wil's laughter gave him a rush of satisfaction. He shut the rear door, pulled the cuff of his jacket over the heel of his hand to buff out the child-sized hand prints from the black Duco, then rounded the car to pull open the front passenger door and climbed in.

"Ready?" His seat belt buckle clicked to lock.

Wil still stood at the driver's side. Door wide open. "Ah..."

"Driven a four-wheel drive before?"

"Sort of. I learned to drive in a beat-up old Jeep on the estate on Devon. It's been a while though, and I'm not familiar with these roads."

Estate in Devon? He really needed to take a closer look at Wil's file. If he was going to trust the man with his family's safety, he probably ought to know more. Maybe even request a security check from his own security service, rather than relying on the butler agency's screening.

But Rhys had learned the hard way to trust his gut.

His gut said Wil—with all his coltish gawkiness—was a good person. More than good. He was different. He belonged at Buck House and Buckle Up Productions with all the other wacky outcasts that Rhys called family.

He twisted to check on Syd and Lex in the back seat. "Everyone ready?"

"Yes, *Dad*," they chorused back.

"Excellent." He raised a questioning eyebrow to Wil. "Looks like we're good to go."

"Right. Good. Excellent." Wil nervously adjusted the mirrors and slid the seat backward a smidge. "I just need directions."

"At the end of Oak Tree Lane, take a right."

"Okay."

The hesitancy in Wil's voice didn't inspire confidence, but Rhys was careful not to show it, gripping his thigh instead of the oh-shit bar as Wil bunny-hopped into first gear. He slowly completed the wide turning circle and neared the gate, where Rhys flicked a button on the windscreen visor and the gate opened toward them.

"Onward, ho," came Syd's high-pitched voice from the rear.

"Onward, ho," Rhys parroted.

"Onward," Lex said. "There's no way I'm saying 'ho'."

"You just did, dork."

"Shut up, nerd."

Wil leaned a few inches sideways till their shoulders almost brushed. "Family tradition?"

"Something like that."

They drove in near silence through the early-evening gloom. Syd and Lex were occupied in the back on their electronic devices, and all Rhys had to give was an occasional directing gesture to Wil as the car ate up the miles along the winding back lanes through the idyllic Oxfordshire countryside.

Calm descended. Which surprised Rhys. It usually took isolating himself in his treehouse to achieve that level of tranquillity.

Was Wil the surprise source of it?

Please, sir, can I have some more?

"Head on up to the green and find a park," Rhys said as they entered a small village. "We'll grab a bite to eat at The Lamb and Lion."

"Will Mark be there?" Syd piped up.

"Don't know, Syd. Let's ask his mum when we get in." He turned to explain to Wil, "Syd's good friends with the pub owner's son. He's a day boy at The Maxwell School."

Rugged up against the descending evening cold, they dashed into the pub and found a corner booth near the roaring open fire. Rhys' cheeks tingled with the sudden change in temperature.

"Hi there, Mr Buckley." The server handed out menus and pointed to a chalkboard with the day's specials written up in a colourful loopy script. "Come up to the bar whenever you're ready to order."

"Thank you. What'll you two have?" Rhys asked Syd and Lex.

"Pizza," Syd slid straight back out of the booth, ducked under the bar leaf, and disappeared into the back rooms of the pub.

"Fish and chips, please," Lex said before also taking off.

"I think I'll have the roast lamb and a half pint of stout. Might as well take advantage of being driven. What about you, Wil?"

"The pulled pork sounds good. And a glass of ginger ale." Wil went to slide off the bench seat, but Rhys stopped him.

"Where are you going?"

Wil pointed at the bar. "To order."

"No. You're on the clock. Which means I pay."

Wil didn't rest back. He pressed his hand flat on the laminated menu on the table. "Exactly. I'm on the clock, which means I do the work. Which means I can put in your order while you relax."

Rhys grasped Wil's wrist and squeezed lightly. "I'm not a pompous twat in a cravat, Wil. I don't need a servant to take care of my every whim." He didn't give a shit who ordered their meals, but it felt wrong for Wil to think he needed to bow and scrape and be on every second of every day. At that rate, he'd burn out before Christmas.

Wil looked down to where they were joined, and his frown deepened.

At first, Rhys couldn't tell if he'd upset Wil, or...what? The man was too stiff for his own good.

What would it take to loosen him up?

Rhys didn't have too long to wonder, because Wil's expression smoothed and a sparkle came to his eye. "Twat in a cravat?" He snorted, his free hand covering his mouth. "Oh, my God. That is legendary. Wait. I have to share." He yanked his hand from Rhys' grip and twisted to pull his phone from his back pocket. He thumbed the screen. "Jane's going to have kittens."

Jane? "Who's Jane?" Wil's girlfriend? Rhys' throat tightened.

"Oh, ah...*Plain Jane* is a forum for people in domestic service professions. We call each other Jane. For confidentiality reasons.

Not that anyone ever posts anything incriminating on it. Mostly, it's funny memes and advice on things like how to get red jelly stains out of carpet—heads up, you can't." He chuckled as his thumbs raced over the screen. Then he paused and looked up. "Is it okay if I share? It's totally anonymous. They won't know who I am, and I won't put your name to it. Promise."

"Go ahead." Annoyed with himself for getting so hung up on a throwaway line, Rhys let go of Wil's wrist and waved his approval. So what if their conversation had felt private? His relationship with Wil was professional. Not personal. And it needed to stay that way.

He schooled his expression and slid out of the booth. "Since you don't have access to a household account yet, I'll go order and pay. Pork and ginger ale, yes?"

The frown flickered again. "Oh. Ah. Yes. Thank you."

"No problem. Be right back."

Returning with two pints, glistening with condensation. He took a deep slog of rich stout and licked the foam from his upper lip. Time to get real about the fact that he had a stranger in his midst. "So, Wil, tell me about yourself." He encouraged.

"Most everything important about me is on my CV."

"That can't be right. No life fits so neatly in stark black and white. You grew up in Devon, right? North or south?"

"North. On the western border of Exmoor National Park."

"Do you have siblings?"

"No. My parents married late and didn't expect to have children. I was a surprise."

"A happy one, I hope?"

"Oh, yes. Absolutely."

"What about cousins?"

"No, none."

"Wow. All alone in the world."

"My parents are alive and kicking, so I'm hardly alone."

"They're still in Devon?" Wil nodded. "And how long were you in London?"

"Two years. Didn't you read my file?" Wil asked incredulously.

Rhys shrugged. "Jacob short-listed a few of you. Then I trusted my gut."

"Wow. That's...I don't even know what that is."

In the awkward silence, they both sipped at their drinks. Wil's eyes dashed about. But Rhys had the opposite problem. He stared at Wil, unable to look away. He had a classic look about him—fine-featured, with a perfectly styled dark blonde quiff, dove grey eyes, and well-groomed stubble. His elegance made Rhys feel positively barbaric.

"What about you?" Wil asked. "You must have at least one sibling. Since your niece and nephew exist."

"They're my sister's kids. Miriam. You may meet her. We don't expect her till Christmas. Occasionally, she shows up without warning. Although that does depend on where she's treading the boards."

"Boards?"

"Miriam's a stage actor. She comes and goes from theatres all over Britain." He paused, amazed that he'd told Wil such personal information. How had the man slipped under his guard so easily? "That's privileged, by the way. The press would have a field day if they knew Miriam Webster was my sister. Or the other way around." He took another sip of his stout, then carefully placed the pint glass dead centre on his coaster. Giving Wil time to recognise the name.

"Miriam Webster? *The* Miriam Webster? Winner of, like, four BAFTA awards? Are you serious?"

"Five, actually. At last count."

"Wow."

"Yeah. She credits anonymity as the cornerstone of her success. That's why she uses a stage name. Says the family name prevents her from being recognised for her talent."

"Because of your fame?"

"More because of our parents. She takes after them. Craves the limelight. Lives happily out of a suitcase."

"Hmm." Wil was quiet for a moment. Probably trying to make sense of the Buckley family tree. "They look like you," he said.

"Who?"

"Syd and Lex." Wil waved a hand around his own face. "The cheekbones."

Rhys already knew that, but it never failed to make him feel good to know others saw the resemblance.

"How often do Lex and Syd return to Buck House?"

Rhys licked the beer foam from his upper lip. "Every school break, and the occasional weekend during term. Angel fusses over them and does their laundry. Plus, I miss them," he admitted.

"Aww. That's sweet."

"Shut up."

Jesus. Why the hell am I flirting?

Probably because it felt like a date—just the two of them, alone in the corner booth by the cosy fire. All they needed was a bottle of red wine and a string quartet.

Ugh.

Shut up, imagination.

"Miriam usually shows up for some of the break. Otherwise, they love going to summer camps in America. Syd—my budding engineer—is in heaven at a science and technology camp near NASA's Cape Canaveral. Lex has been going to the same lakeside camp in Upstate New York since she was nine. She loves to share a cabin with her girlfriends. It's incredible to hear them together—like they're speaking another language.

"Kids."

"Ha! You sound middle-aged. You can't be much over twenty yourself."

"I'm twenty-two, soon to be twenty-three."

"God, you're a baby."

"Am not."

Rhys snorted, totally entertained. "I rest my case."

Wil straightened in his seat. "Well, how old are you?"

"Thirty-three and a third," Rhys kept a straight face. Just. Then ruined it all, cracking a grin. "You'll do, Mr Haines."

Wil hummed, clearly pleased with himself. "What about your parents?"

"What about them?"

"Are they still around?"

"Alive, yes. Around, no." The word came out blunt. Revealing the secret of his sister's identity was one thing. Spilling details of their sad-sack, lonely childhood? That was a story best left in the dust. As luck would have it, a server arrived with their meals, and the kids, seconds behind. Rhys breathed a sigh of relief.

He was so used to it just being him and Lex and Syd, taking on the world, that adding Wil to the mix felt surreal. Not quite a nuclear family—mother, father, daughter, son—but pretty damn close.

Lex slurped the tail end of her strawberry milkshake and sat back with a groan. "Food coma." She fluttered her eyelashes dramatically.

Like mother, like daughter.

"All done?" He could have stayed there all night, but the kids had to get to school after their half-term break, and he had work to do back home. "Great, then let's get on the road."

"Do we really have to go?" Syd whined.

"Yes, we really do."

"Can we come home next weekend?" Asked Lex.

"No, for the fourteen-gazillionth time. I have meetings at Pinewood. Besides, you'll get back to the dorm, find your friends, and forget all about me. Then it'll be me whining about not getting to see you. Poor Wil will be left with a teary boss, and Wil doesn't want that, do you, Wil?"

"Um, no?"

"Exactly. Now, no more whinging. Scoot."

They shuffled out of the booth and pulled on their puffy coats. Braving the cold, their breath blew clouds into the night air as they hustled to the car.

"Take a right up there to get back on the back road to Oxford. On the drive home, I'll point out a few local landmarks."

"Like the Rose and Crown," interjected Lex.

"Yes, like the Rose and Crown. That's the pub in Cantnoor Cross," he explained to Wil. "A few of my mates like to get a pint there on a Sunday afternoon. There's nothing wrong with being neighbourly, Alexandra. But I was thinking more of the private airfield, and the riding school, and the train station."

"Sounds like trains, planes, and automobiles," said Wil.

"And horses," said Lex.

"And horses." Wil nodded to Lex in the rear-view mirror.

"Do you ride?" Rhys asked.

"I *have* ridden. Once. A badger spooked my pony, and I flew off." He shuddered. "Never again."

"What's a badger?" asked Syd.

"It's a small, furry animal with black and white stripes."

"Like a skunk? Did it stink you?"

"No, badgers don't do that. Thank goodness."

"Did you get back on?" Typical Syd, asking a million questions.

Wil gripped the wheel tighter, his hands making scratching sounds on the leather. "Yes. Apparently, you should always get back on the horse. Or in this case, the pony. That's the rule. According to my...friend."

"Not a friend anymore?" Rhys guessed.

"No."

"Because he made you get back on the horse?"

"Among other reasons."

In other words, mind your own damn business, Buckley.

There was a story there. He wanted to ask more. But with the kids in the car, listening avidly, he had to respect Wil's right to privacy. "Fair enough."

In the rear vision mirror, he could see Syd squirrelling about in his seat.

"Did you go to the bathroom back at the pub?"

"Uncle Rhys!" Syd whined with embarrassment.

"Uncle Rhys?"

"Yes, Lex."

"How long is Wil going to be staying?"

"As long as he's needed."

"But we won't need him in the summer, will we? Mum will be home and we can all be together properly."

"Wil isn't around for your benefit, Lex. He's there to help run Buck House after Jacob graduates."

"And because Evangeline is knocked up."

"Alexandra! Don't ever use language like that about anyone."

"Well, it's true."

"It doesn't matter if it's true or not. It's rude."

"Sorry, Uncle Rhys," she mumbled.

"What's 'knocked up' mean Uncle Rhys?"

Rhys groaned. "Never mind, Syd. Just know that you should never say that about anyone."

"It means she's pregnant."

"That's enough, Alexandra."

An awkward silence descended and the icy darkness of the night seemed to seep into the car. He guided Wil off the A road toward the impressive gate at the entrance to The Maxwell School.

To show the guard his ID, Rhys had to lean across Wil. It barely took a second, but one whiff of the man's crisp, clean scent had him wishing for a two-man sleeping bag and a clear night under the stars.

Stuff that imagination back in its bag, Buckley.

He was going to get himself in trouble if he wasn't careful.

Past the gate, Wil drove along the winding oak-lined drive at don't-run-over-the-children speed and up to the original Edwardian schoolhouse, perched on a natural rise.

"Where is everyone?" Rhys asked.

"Dinner," Lex succinctly replied, already tumbling out of the back seat. "Bye!" she hollered as she grabbed her gear and dashed up the stairs to the front doors.

So much for being in a food coma.

"I expected it to be bigger," Wil ventured.

"Most of it's tucked into the slope behind the original building. Makes it difficult for paparazzi to get their lenses on the students."

"I guess a lot of the kids here would have high-profile parents."

"Yeah. Makes them targets everywhere they go. About fifteen years ago, a boy was kidnapped from the front grounds of the school."

"Wow. Brazen."

"Yeah. It was years before I enrolled Lex, of course. And they've stepped up security in a major way since then. But that sort of danger is never far from my mind."

Wil twisted to look over his shoulder at Syd. A look of concern on his face.

"Don't worry about him hearing. I don't keep that sort of thing from my kids. If Syd or Lex came to harm, and I hadn't prepared them..." *how do you spell 'worst nightmare?'* "It's my job to keep them safe. Not ignorant."

"Has anyone ever threatened your children?"

"No. Touch wood. The Maxwell School is vigilant, and Buck House has a comprehensive security system. Don't worry, though, they're not your concern."

Wil's gaze whipped back to him. Sharp eyes catching the light. "They're yours. They belong to Buck House. That makes them mine to worry about."

Dumbfounded. Rhys stared back at him. It was so total. How could anyone be one-hundred percent committed in so little time? To people he barely knew? Could Rhys trust someone who could flick that switch so readily?

"Uncle Rhys?"

"Yes, mate?"

"Can we go?"

"Oh. Ah. Yeah. Yeah, of course."

"Sorry." Wil threw the car into gear. "Where to?"

"Continue around the manor. There's a drop off spot in front of the Junior School dorms. I need to sign Syd in directly."

After pulling up outside the rabbit warren of gated buildings, he and Syd slipped out into the cold. "Come with us if you like. It'll be useful to register your details with the House Master on the off chance that I need you to pick up the kids some time."

"Okay."

The car's lights flashed as Wil clicked the electronic lock and they made their way together, through the archway and into the flagstone central courtyard of the triple-story brick building. It thronged with kids and their parents and luggage.

"Bye!" Syd raced past him, his school backpack dangling heavy from his small shoulders.

"Love you too, Syd." Rhys called after.

He felt Wil's presence come up beside him and, for a second, Rhys pretended he and Wil were a couple. Partners. Husbands, maybe. Delivering their children to school.

What would they do after?

Head into Oxford for a romantic night punt on the Thames?

Lug blankets and a quart of scotch up Coombe Hill and lie out under the stars?

Head back to Buck House to enjoy the privacy of their re-claimed home?

Yes. That.

Door number three, please, Monty.

"Where should I put these?" Wil asked.

"Huh?" The film reel of coupledom dissolved.

They weren't a couple.

There was nothing romantic about their connection.

Nothing at all.

Rhys rolled his neck and did his best not to look at Wil. Fantasising was one thing. He'd built his business on that skill. Getting hard over the idea of him and his butler getting cosy? That was just wrong.

He cast a quick glance over to where Syd was entrenched with his friends. "Let's go see the Junior House Master."

Wil filled his details into the giant leather-bound ledger and signed his name. "This feels like a Dickens novel."

"Ha! Not a novel thought. Pun intended." He smirked at Wil's groan. "Come on. Let's get out of here."

"Don't you need to say goodbye to Syd?"

"Nah. Not much point interrupting that merry band of mini-misfits."

He pressed his gloved hand to the flat of Wil's back and guided him back toward the car.

Too forward?

Didn't each layer of clothing nullify his touch? Glove. Coat. Sweater. Shirt.

Four layers ought to be enough.

As they approached the Range Rover, Wil stepped away from Rhys' hand—the key fob jangling metal-harsh as he pulled it from his coat pocket. "You still want me to drive?"

It was tempting to take the keys. To keep his hands out of trouble. But why fix what wasn't broken? "Sure," he said, and swerved around to the passenger side of the Range Rover. "I'll point out the sights on the way home."

"Guess that means I passed the test."

"Test?" What the hell was Wil talking about?

"The 'can Wil drive safely?' test."

"Ah. Yes. Congratulations. Wil can drive. Although, with Syd and Lex on board, I would have stopped you within fifty feet of Buck House if I thought they were at risk."

"Thank you, Sir."

Sir? "Geez, Wil. That's worse than calling me Mr Buckley. Can we agree from now on that in all circumstances, I am Rhys?"

"Hmm...not sure if I can do that."

"Well, try."

"What if you're having tea with royalty?"

"I don't care if we're picnicking with the Queen of Sheba. I am Rhys. You are Wil. If you stick to that, we are going to get along just fine."

"I don't think the Queen of Sheba is alive..."

"I don't care. Repeat after me, 'I am Rhys, and you are Wil'."

"I am Rhys..."

Grr...

"Fine. *You* are Rhys. *I* am Wil. And *we* are going to get along just fine."

"Excellent." Rhys tapped the cold dashboard. "Take me home, Jeeves."

Wil snickered. "Nice re-appropriation of pop culture. Even if it is a bit retro."

"An oldie, but a goodie. Glad to hear you appreciate the finer arts."

"It's on auto-repeat on *Plain Jane*."

"Ah. Of course."

A comfortable silence descended. Til Wil piped up and said, "I've got a better one."

"What's that?" He'd almost forgotten their train of conversation.

"Onward ho."

"Ha! Yes. Now you truly are part of the Buckley tribe."

Chapter 5

Wil

Wil watched the pink and orange streaks of sunrise punch through the thick morning fog and glisten on the frost that edged the kitchen windows.

He wanted to enjoy the dreamlike stillness of the chilly morning, but nervous energy thrummed through his body. Jacob would arrive soon and offer a host of sage advice. Bravery and a little brain food were all he needed to kick things off. So, he threw a few dry logs into the Aga and watched as the banked coals caught and new flames leaped to life. He shut the door and twisted the air vent open a smidgen to encourage the coals, then filled the kettle for his morning cup of tea. While he waited for the water to boil, he pulled out his pocket notebook and began a fresh to-do list.

Half a page later, Wil poured steaming water over the Earl Grey tea leaves. The scent of bergamot permeated the air, and he sighed into the gentle quiet.

Heaven.

He rooted out locally laid organic eggs to make a scrambled concoction. After a quick whisk, he poured the eggs onto the hot-to-touch skillet and stirred gently, added a tiny knob of butter, then scooped the sheeny eggs into a stone-ware bowl, finishing them with a crack of pepper and fresh herbs from the windowsill.

He perched his arse on the warm edge of the Aga and dug in. "Yum."

Moments later, the back door opened, bringing with it a rush of cold, damp air. "Shit," Jacob stomped on the rough doormat, grumbling to himself as he tried to dislodge mud from his shoes. "Oops. Apologies for the French, Wil."

"*Pas de problème, monsieur. Voulez-vous des oeufs?*"

Jacob pulled off his hat. "Oofs?"

"Eggs." Wil tilted his bowl to show the last bite of scrambled eggs.

"Oh, no thanks. Wouldn't say no to a coffee, though. Have you figured out the beast yet?" he pointed at the espresso machine.

Wil held up a finger, finished his last bite of breakfast, rinsed the bowl in the sink, then approached the shiny silver espresso machine that had enough bells and whistles to rival a steam locomotive. "Just don't make me call it the beast until I've mastered it and it can no longer undermine my authority."

I will not be intimidated.

Jacob chuckled. "That's the ticket. Show it who's boss, Wil."

He clanked around for a while with the grinder, the tamp, and the steamer, and came out with a beverage that looked greyer than the North Sea.

"Hmm. Something tells me I didn't win."

Jacob's choked laugh was all the impetus Wil needed to back away from the machine. "I give up. Rhys calls you Mage, doesn't he? Teach me, oh wise one."

"Difficult, coffee is."

Fifteen minutes later, after wasting at least a pint of milk, far too many grounds, and risking third-degree steam burns, Wil finally created a latte that met Jacob's requirements...just.

"You'll thank me when Rhys doesn't spit out your first offering."

"I'm already inclined to thank you. Don't worry, pride won't stop me from accepting help."

Jacob nodded. "That's good, because your job will be varied, multifaceted, elaborate, and unexpected."

"All that, huh?"

"Drama is a given around here. It's not possible to be prepared for every eventuality, so you might as well get used to asking for help. Don't worry, though. You're not the only one needing to learn."

"I'm not?"

"Word is Rhys is to be offered a King's Honour. He's going to need guidance that I can't give."

"Seriously? That's incredible."

Jacob's voice hardened. "He well and truly deserves it. Rhys has contributed to the British film industry for a very long time. He's proved himself ten times over."

"Oh, I didn't mean that he doesn't deserve it. I'm sure he does. It's just that..." What did he mean? "Just that it's amazing. A King's honour. That's...wow."

"As I said, he deserves it. And he'll need your support."

Such loyalty. It was rare. Wil had to respect it.

He straightened to stand tall and looked Jacob in the eye. Man to man. "He'll have it. I promise. You can trust me."

Jacob stared back at him for a long moment. "Good," he said, then glanced down at his coffee cup. "Maybe not with the coffee quite yet, but we can work on that. Let's get to work."

With Jacob's help, Wil began to clarify his role at Buck House, conscious that eventually he'd need to take the lead.

"The appointment book I've been keeping will give you some structure and help with forward planning. Rhys takes care of his office, but there are folders here on the care and maintenance of the house and studio, respectively, and another on events. Rhys holds seasonal dinner parties when he's in residence."

"In residence? Sounds like royalty. Does he have a flag that goes up when he's 'at home'?" Wil joked.

Jacob groaned. "Don't even suggest it. Rhys' ego is big enough already."

"A coat of arms with a buck and a teddy bear?"

"Even better." Jacob laughed along with the joke. "You'll do, Mr Haines."

That took Wil aback. "That's exactly what Rhys said last night. Word for word."

"Guess we chose well, then. Now. Getting back to the themed parties. These are going to be your babies to organise. Rhys likes to invite a mix of people from his circle of friends and from the local area."

"How many people?"

"The dining table seats twenty-four, but we usually cap it at about twenty."

"And he doesn't engage a party planner?"

"No. You'll have Calder the chef, and he usually brings someone to help serve. Evangeline also helps with the cooking, but she's not as nimble these days."

"What themes have already been done?"

Jacob pointed to the annual files in the cabinet. "Have a look. I usually ask the kids to help me out. They're always full of ideas. We all enjoyed the Halloween party put on by the local pub last weekend. But I think the best dinner party themes in recent years have been: down the rabbit hole; mergers and acquisitions; and dodgy rockers."

"Mergers and acquisitions?" Wil asked.

"The Chilterns are riddled with new money. The banker set. We thought the connection was obvious, but many couples surprised us by coming dressed up as honeymooners. Get it? Mergers and Acquisitions?" He waggled his eyebrows. "It gave everyone an excuse to behave badly in dark corners."

"Hmm. Clever. How about the 70s, or 20s flappers? Villains and vigilantes? Silent-era screen sirens? Under the sea? Pirates?" Wil's mind spun from one theme to another.

"You can do whatever theme you like. I usually start with a theme, then find guests to fit. Unless Rhys wants a particular guest to attend. Then I have to find a theme to fit. Rhys gravitates toward clever and creative." He smirked cheekily. "No pressure."

"No pressure, huh?"

"He's actually pretty easy to please. If everything is running smoothly, he'll leave you to it. I hope you don't mind isolation because there will be many days that you'll not see another soul. Not even each other."

"I think I can cope with that. I'm not easily bored."

"Okay, then. Let's rug up and head outside."

Wil stretched with relief. "Great. I haven't had an opportunity to explore much further that the house."

"The woods around here are amazing. They're beautiful any time of year, but at the tail end of spring, the valleys erupt in a carpet of bluebells."

"Sounds magical."

"Oh, it is. Make sure you take some time this week to explore the local woodland trails. The garden is gated for privacy, but Rhys' land is extensive, and there are dozens of public footpaths that criss-cross the surrounding hills and valleys. You can't go wrong." Jacob took him out the front door and pointed at the massive four-door, two-story structure adjacent to Buck House. "That's the studio."

"Really? I thought it was the garage." It wasn't unusual for wealthy people to own half a dozen toys on wheels.

"Originally, yes. You'll see why we call it the studio in a minute." Jacob punched a code into a security keypad and rolled open one of the middle doors.

Immediately, Wil understood what he meant.

The Range Rover and a sportier Audi occupied one end. The remaining interior was a double-storey warehouse with simple partitions that differentiated storage areas from work areas. Hundreds of black reinforced boxes, like those roadies used to haul music equipment, were piled high between plastic-sheathed furniture and racks of costumes. The towering wall at the back was painted green, and the floor in front of it was marked with cryptic tape marks resembling hieroglyphs.

Above the two cars was a mezzanine floor, accessible by a spiral staircase. When Jacob led him up it, Wil saw it was split into two zones—a collaborative workspace in the front and an editing suite in the rear. "It's sound and light proof and equipped with all the editing gadgets and gizmos." Jacob waved at the mysterious array of lights and knobs and slides on the electronic table. "You'll have to ask Rhys for an explanation if you want to know what they do. I have no idea."

"This is where he works?" Wil asked.

"Most of the Buckle Up Productions employees are based at the office in London, but Rhys likes to work from home, so most of his visitors will need to come here. He never takes them to his private office. Don't ever let anyone convince you they're allowed up there."

"Isn't this his office?"

"No. That's outside, in the oak tree."

Wil must have heard him wrong. "In a tree?"

"Treehouse."

"That's...novel. Where?"

"In the backyard." Jacob said, as though it was perfectly normal for a man to have his office in a tree. "He rarely allows anyone up there. It's his *space of grace*, as he calls it. Some kind of Zen thing that he picked up years ago. Don't take it personally if he never invites you into that inner sanctum. Even Lex and Syd need special permission."

"Have he ever invited you?"

"Once. Sort of. I got to the top rung of the ladder when a brilliant idea struck him and wouldn't let me up any further."

"Ooo-kay then, no excursions to the treehouse."

"He calls it his office, to head off the curious. We like to keep it a secret from the outside world, but you've probably already seen the lights on in the tree, since it's right across from your attic balcony."

He hadn't, no. But then Wil had been exhausted when he climbed the stairs to his rooms the previous night, on a fast-track journey for bed.

Leaving the studio, Jacob led him around the side of the house to where he could get an easy vantage of Wil's Juliette balcony and Rhys' treehouse.

"I can hardly believe I didn't notice it earlier." The thinning autumn foliage did little to camouflage the suspended structure.

"Don't be surprised if his lights are on through the night. It's his creative flow time, as he calls it. I sometimes wonder if he and the owls are hatching plans together."

"You mentioned Zen."

"Yeah. Either way, it's a no-go zone."

Wil chuckled. "No entering the arboreal sanctum. Check. Any other rules?"

"Not really. Keep the noise down in the mornings, since he's up all night and usually sleeps till about noon. You don't have to work in silence, but remember his bedroom is above our office, so close the window and door if you're doing anything noisy before noon. Making a phone call. Anything like that.

Most people know not to contact him in the morning. It's only the couriers who have an annoying habit of coming early and ringing the visitor's bell. I try to monitor the main gate security feed through my tablet, but I'm not always quick enough to catch them before they ring the bell."

Jacob passed the kitchen door to where a beautiful dry-stone wall separated the lawn from the fallow vegetable garden. He patted the cold stone. "This is one of Rhys' summer projects from a few years back. He learnt to dry-stone like a pro." Jacob pointed at the woods on the opposite side of the garden. "And down there in the valley is his and Syd's current pride and joy."

"All I see are trees."

"The jungle gym is pretty well camouflaged. It's a run of ropes, monkey bars, and balance posts. Everything a budding Tarzan could want." He gave an idle shrug. "I doubt the estate's insurance company would approve it, but what they don't know about they can't condemn, so..."

"Sounds like fun...for somebody else."

Jacob raised a brow in query.

"Once a klutz, always a klutz."

"Ah. Sorry 'bout that."

"Remember that movie *Billy Elliot?*"

"Of course. A British classic."

"I wanted to be Billy so bad. He was my hero."

A smile lurked on Jacob's lips. "Why do I feel like there's a story here?"

"Not just a story. A tragedy. When I told my mother I wanted to take dance lessons, she laughed so hard." It made him a little sick to remember.

"Burn."

"Exactly."

They both stared out into the gloom beneath the trees.

"You've got the right name, though. Billy…William…Wil."

"Yeah. You'd think it was meant to be, right? Alas…"

"Not your fate?"

"Most definitely not. I can walk in a straight line, no problem, but the minute I try to spin around, everything goes to pot."

"That is tragic. I'm sorry."

"Don't be. I have other strengths."

"Well, don't hurt yourself, but have a go at the jungle gym in your free time. It's a great workout. Rhys started exercising down there after he spent three straight months in the editing suite. Looked positively vampiric. It didn't take long for him to take on some colour and buff up a bit."

"Strengthens your core," came a voice from behind, making Wil nearly leap out of his skin.

He looked around, then up, into the tree, where Rhys held open one of the small, porthole windows. Wil could only see the upper half of his torso, but, wearing only a t-shirt, his defined biceps were clear for the world to see. He looked strong in a loose-limbed runner kind of way.

Buff indeed.

"Did you sleep up there?" Wil's voice rose about three octaves.

"Don't sleep much through the night. But that's not what us vampires do best."

Jacob looked abashed for a second, then glared up at Rhys. "No lurking allowed. House rule."

"Me? I'm just minding my own business, in my own space."

"I thought you said there weren't any more house rules?" Wil couldn't help teasing.

Rhys snorted. "He's got you there. Getting the lay of the land?" He asked Wil.

"It's a beautiful property, Mr Buckley."

His dark eyes turned fierce. "I thought we resolved this yesterday? I'm Rhys. He's Jacob. You're Wil. And I *am* making that a new house rule." With that, he disappeared from the window.

Jacob leaned in close to whisper. "Give him caffeine, and you'll be set."

"Is he always this hot and cold?"

"Hot, huh?" Jacob quirked his brow, and Wil blushed.

"Not like that."

Exactly like that.

"He'll get used to you. It's more the idea of having a stranger around the house. Privacy is very important to him."

"I can understand that. But my job is to make his life smooth, not more difficult."

"He'll see that in the end. Just give him time. Show him you won't intrude and he'll gradually come to believe it."

"I can do that."

"The alternative is to become indispensable. He won't kick you out if you're essential to his happiness."

Happiness?

Wil frowned. It wasn't too hard to imagine ways he could do that—none of them part of his job description. "A tall order."

"You'll do your best, though, right?"

"Always."

"That's all I we ask for. Anyway, that's the full tour. Time for a hot drink, I think. Come on." He winked. "The beast awaits."

"Oh, joy."

Chapter 6

Wil

Surviving the first two days on the job was cause for celebration as far as Wil was concerned, even if he had made an arse of himself on more than one occasion.

The house quiet, he fixed a steaming bowl of Evangeline's delicious tomato and basil soup and a cheese toasty, carried them up to his attic rooms, kicked off his shoes, and curled up on his new sofa to eat. It wasn't the crowded bars his twenty-something friends gravitated to, but that didn't matter. Solitude had never bothered him. And it wasn't as though he was entirely alone. Beyond his dim reflection in the French doors, Wil could make out a silhouette in one of the small windows in the treehouse outside.

Rhys.

Wil put the last of his dinner aside and crossed his room to get a closer look.

Rhys was still, for the most part. His head tilted down. His mouth moving. Was he speaking to someone? Voicing lines of dialogue? Whatever he was saying, he did it with intensity.

When Rhys turned a certain way, the golden light in the treehouse highlighted the sharp angles of his cheekbone and the straight brows that guarded his ocean-deep eyes. When he turned the other way, the sharp angles became messy curls.

Gorgeous, Wil thought.

And not for me.

Pachelbel's Canon rang out from his phone, interrupting the analysis of his boss' attributes, and bringing him down to earth.

"Hi, Mum." The ringtone was an easy giveaway.

"Hello, dear. How was your day?"

"Good."

"You don't sound so sure."

"No, it was good. Quieter than expected. Compared to yesterday, that is."

"What happened yesterday?"

"We took the children to school."

"They don't expect you to babysit, do they?" Mrs Haines was nothing if not clear about who did what in a proper household.

"No. You know how important it is to become familiar with the family and their particular ways."

"True. Just don't get trapped into taking care of the children. That's the nanny's responsibilities. Remember what your father always says—"

"Be the rock."

"Exactly. Your job is to be the bedrock of the house. The butler must maintain his dignity."

"Or her dignity."

"Pardon?"

"There are female butlers too, you know. Some of the best butlers are women. And I hardly think caring for children is beneath me."

She ignored that. "Are the other staff manageable?"

"There aren't all that many staff. Just a personal assistant and a housekeeper." His mother did not need to know that both Jacob and Evangeline were due to leave within the month.

"No nanny? Who's looking after the children?"

"They're school age, Mum. And they go to boarding school through each term."

"Well, that may be so, but a house still needs to be properly run, and you can't be expected to do everything."

The urge to defend his boss came on strong. Rhys was an excellent father...er...uncle. He was kind and attentive, and he obviously cared deeply for his niece and nephew.

"So, what have you and Dad been up to?"

"Oh, you know. The usual. Nothing much changes around here."

"That's not true." He loved Devon. The wild land. The tight community. The only thing missing was opportunity. He'd left for London with grand dreams, sure that after completing his diploma he'd walk straight into a position in a rich pile of a country home with a full host of servants to lead. A place just like Mistlethwaite Manor. A place to make his mark. To prove himself.

But that was before he'd struck out in twenty-seven bloody interviews.

Buck House, with its cosy scale and quirky family, was nothing like the position he'd strived for. But something about the place felt right.

Time to discard the past and forge a new future.

"Who is this Mr Buckley, Wil?"

"I doubt you'd have heard of him. He's a director and producer."

"In the theatre? Oh, dear. You must be careful of those West End types. Very flighty."

"Film, Mum. He has his own production company."

"Cinema?" Condescension dripped through the phone.

"He's highly respected in the industry."

"Well, that may be, dear, but..."

"And he's raising two children. They're very close."

"Well, there is that. And it is good to hear that he's a family man. Children should always be a priority. How old did you say they are, Wil?"

"You know I can't give you details. Not if I want the family to trust me." In fact, he shouldn't have told her what he had. Even if he hadn't signed an ironclad confidentiality agreement, Rhys deserved privacy.

"Oh absolutely, dear. Very wise of you. I'm just a trifle concerned that this man might not be an acceptable employer. He has no history; no family to speak of."

None listed in Debrett's.

"And if, as you say, he's a popular artist, he'll be in the tabloids. He'll have fans and, oh my goodness, he may even have stalkers."

"Mother." Wil groaned. "This is not Hollywood."

"Well, of course not, dear. British journalists are no doubt much better behaved—"

"That's not what I meant."

"But you know all those film types are into drugs and debauchery."

"Drugs and debauchery?" He had to laugh at that. "Mother, Mr Buckley is a perfectly normal, perfectly respectable, and perfectly trustworthy man, who runs a successful production company from his home. As for the rest, you've always said that no man should need a title or crest to be a gentleman."

"Well, of course not, dear. And, as you say, he is a respected businessman."

"Exactly." His patience worn thin, Wil sighed loud enough for his mother to hear. The passive aggression was most definitely beneath his dignity, but he didn't want to hear anything more said about Rhys.

"You know how proud we are of you, Wil. I just want you to be safe."

"I know, Mum. I'm safe here. I promise."

"So long as you're careful."

"Always. He's a good man, Mum." He stifled a yawn. "Thanks for the call, but I have to go. It's been a long day. Will you pass on my love to Dad?"

"Of course, dear. You take care."

"Goodnight," he said. His mother might've returned the farewell, but Wil didn't hear it. His focus had drifted down from the stars above to the gleaming windows in the tree, where, barely ten feet away, Rhys Buckley, in the flesh, stared directly at him.

Shit. Had Rhys heard him?

Look away, Wil.

But he couldn't. And when Rhys gave a jazz-hand wave, Wil did it too. It was like one of those silly mirror-image parlour tricks. But nothing about them was the same. They were boss and butler. The client and the help. He and Rhys might mirror each other temporarily, but they lived in entirely different worlds.

If Wil was going to succeed, he had to remember that fact.

Chapter 7

Wil

"How's your day going?" Evangeline hollered over the milk-frothing steam engine.

"So far, I've been more doorman than butler. I've never seen so many couriers, nor signed my name so many times in a single day." He massaged his wrist. "Celebrities must really struggle to autograph posters and books and...and..." His brain tired, Wil searched for more ideas.

"Skin. Don't forget the fans that want a tattoo of their favourite celeb's signature."

"Is that actually a thing?"

"Sure. Just ask Rhys."

"Someone tattooed his name? On their skin? Seriously?"

"It's not as uncommon as you might think. Rhys is talented and loaded and gorgeous. What's not to obsess over?"

"Indeed." Industry consensus claimed Rhys was talented. He was loaded. And Wil only had to look with his own eyes to confirm that his boss was gorgeous. But, "Obsession? That's just creepy."

"Rhys rarely covets the spotlight, but he still has to do a lot to maintain privacy and security."

"Yes. I'm getting pretty good at taking stills of every visitor. Luckily, they've all been on the 'acceptable' list Jacob gave me. I haven't had to bring out my tough voice yet."

"Oh, your tough voice. I want to hear that. Do it, now."

He tried to give her a stern frown, but it was impossible to hold, and he waved off Evangeline's mocking laughter. "Do you know who JK Jones is? He, or she, is on the 'acceptable' list, but the innocuous name had me wondering. Jacob impressed upon me the need to be vigilant against the crazies, as he put it, so..."

"Oh, no. Jacky's cool. He's a great foley artist."

"Hmm." He really needed to boost his knowledge of film terminology. Some roles he could figure out. Sound engineer and costume designer were pretty obvious. But foley artist and gaffer? What the heck were they?

He hid his ignorance behind appreciation for the cappuccino. "Mmm. Thanks Evangeline. Ever think about opening your own café? This is delicious."

"My pleasure."

"Well, it's *my* pleasure, actually. But, thanks."

She laughed. "Maybe one day, Wil. Can I count on you as my first customer?"

"Absolutely."

If I'm still here.

Tut, tut, Wil. We're not thinking about that.

Wil stuck his head back in the sand and re-invoked his motto. *Composure and confidence.*

"Can I do anything for you before I hide away in the media room for the rest of the day? Jacob gave me Rhys' films to watch."

"Boning up, hey?" She laughed.

"What? No!" *There will be absolutely no boning in the media room...or...or anywhere.*

Was it wrong that an image of him and Rhys, in the tree-house, naked, sweat-slick limbs writhing with ecstasy, burst to life in his mind? All it was missing was the soundtrack.

Shit.

No boning.

No boning.

No boning the boss.

"Ooo-kay, then." Evangeline rubbed her bump. "Would you get that bag of pecans and the brown sugar down for me? I have a stepladder, but this little one has a tizzy whenever I go high."

"I can do that." Thank God, a simple task. "What are you making?"

"Pecan pie. It's one of Rhys' favourites."

"And mine." He stretched for the sugar and nuts, glad to have a moment to school his expression.

"Thanks."

"Anything else I can do?"

"Hmm. Well. You could take Rhys his coffee. He must have been up all night to have gone through so many beans."

"In his bedroom?" *Hell, no.*

Evangeline laughed again. "No silly. He's in his office." She pointed out the back door. "Just ring the brass bell at the base of the tree. He'll send a basket lift down from his window. Ring the bell again when you've loaded his coffee, and he'll winch it up."

A safe enough distance. "I can do that."

Evangeline handed over the thermos. "Super long, quadruple shot, long black. Send him my love."

"Got it."

"Perfect. Thanks, Wil. Now, don't worry about answering the door while you watch Rhys' films. I can get it till sundown." She swiped and tapped her phone till she had the security feed of the gate camera streaming. "See."

"You're a treasure."

"Ha! That's what I always say."

The chilly breeze snagged his hair as he peered up through the half-naked branches, spying a grey squirrel that twitched with nervous excitement and a pair of twittering sparrows.

The little basket lift was already hanging low, expectant. "You sure do like your caffeine." He loaded the thermos, rang the bell, and watched as the winch beside the window turned to pull it up.

"Thanks, Angel." Came Rhys' distracted call. Then nothing.

Wil went to say, "No, it's me," but he stopped himself as the technicolour image of him and Rhys returned, complete with soundtrack. The ladder was right there. A rustic stairway to heaven within reach.

That thought was the killer. Because even if Rhys did reciprocate the attraction, Wil wouldn't do anything about it...*couldn't* do anything about it.

"Oh, it's you."

Wil jerked, stumbled over one of the tree roots, and fell on his arse on the damp ground. "Shit." He must look like a drunkard. It took all his gumption to look up into the tree, to Rhys' pale face, framed by the round porthole window, one inky brow elevated.

"What?" Wil asked, mortified.

Good job, Wil, go on the offensive.

"Y'right there, mate?"

"I'm fine." He hid his face as he regained his feet. Nothing but time and heat would resolve the wet patch on the arse of his trousers, but Wil brushed at it anyway as the awkward moment stretched out.

Eventually, Rhys broke it with an innocuous, "Thanks for the coffee."

Wil expelled the lungful of air he didn't realise he'd been holding. "You're welcome. I'll just be getting back," he pointed a finger over his shoulder, "To work." *AKA sanity.*

Composure and confidence in short supply, Wil did his best to walk tall as he retraced his steps back to the kitchen door. Of course, walking tall meant he didn't notice the elevated paver just outside the kitchen door. His toe caught its lip, and he tripped, falling forward, just managing to catch himself with a hard slap of his hand against the solid wood door.

"Fuck!" It stung like a belly flop in water.

The slap must have alerted Evangeline, too, because before he could regain his feet, again, she opened the door and he fell on his face on the flagstone floor.

"Jesus, Wil. Are you alright?"

He groaned. "If I said yes, would you leave me alone to my mortification?"

"Probably not."

"Oh. Well then..." It was tempting to stay down, but he pushed up onto his knees, then to stand, hyperaware of every new hurt—especially the one to his pride.

"Let's get you a cup of tea. You'll be needing some fortitude."

Wil brushed the grit from his hands, then shoved them deep in his pockets. "To recover from my embarrassment?"

"Ha! No. To get through all of Rhys' films. Rhys is brilliant, but he does go on. Avoid the Director's Cut editions, and you'll be fine. Go get comfy in the media room. I'll bring in tea and biscuits."

"Thanks, Evangeline. Now I see why Rhys calls you Angel."

"Tosh." She waved him away, and Wil took the stairs two at a time to change into clean trousers before doing just as she'd suggested.

In the cosy media room, he pulled down the block-out blinds, stretched out on one of the luxurious butter-soft leather cinema chairs, and cued up *Saturnine*. Wil was soon caught up in the dark visual wonder of it. According to Rhys' IMDB filmography, he'd been successful with the movie straight out of film school, and the accolades hadn't stopped since. Wil couldn't say he entirely enjoyed the gritty, mind-twisting story of an idiosyncratic, time-travelling detective who caused his own un-birthing, and thus unleashed the time-traveller's paradox, but he'd been riveted, nonetheless. He barely even noticed when Evangeline ghosted in with tea and biscuits.

He flicked through Rhys' five other films. What to watch next?

One game of eeny-meeny-miny-mo later, Wil pressed play on *Cave in My Heart*, billed as a dystopian romance. Two hours later, he was crying like a baby. "For God's sake, Rhys. Haven't you heard of happy?"

Franky's Army wasn't much better. It was interesting to see the streets of London from the perspective of a three-foot tall ruffian, displaced by the second world war, but too many senseless deaths made Wil feel like he needed an emotional decontamination shower—to bathe in nothing but sunshine and rainbows.

How could Rhys stand it?

And what would Wil say—what *could* he say—when Rhys inevitably asked him what he thought about his films?

Should he pretend to like them all?

Go with tact, rather than truth?

Nobody got through butler school without learning to be diplomatic, but it wasn't Wil's strong suit. Subterfuge didn't come naturally.

As the credits rolled on *Franky's Army*, Wil checked the time.

Evangeline had said she usually served dinner at half six. That gave him twenty minutes to put his game face on before he had to face Rhys.

"Tact," he added to his mantra as he took the stairs at a fast clip.

"Composure." Step.

"Confidence." Step.

"Tact." Step.

"Composure, confidence, tact." Step. "Composure, confidence, ta—"

"What's that?"

"—a-a-act." Wil teetered on the second-to-last step. Arms pin-wheeling.

"Woah!" Hands grabbed at Wil's waist. Strong arms wrapped high around his rib-cage, pulled him back from the brink. Reflex made Wil grab, too, and he clung on with tight fists to the soft material that hugged Rhys' chest.

Rhys winced.

"Sorry. Wil untangled his fists from Rhys' shirt and patted his chest. "Didn't mean to rip out your chest hairs."

Did I just say that?

Rhys' mouth did a little twisty quirk, and Wil's stomach flipped.

He looked up to the first-floor landing, searching for either an escape route, instructions to kick start the whole time-traveller thing, or a higher power to save him.

Take me anywhere, Lord. Anywhere but here.

But there wasn't anything up there to see. Just Ted-head's beady eyes staring down at him—judging Wil's idiocy.

Ugh. So much for composure.

"Are you okay?" Rhys asked.

"Of course." *No.*

"Who were you talking to?"

"Nothing. Nobody. I wasn't talking to anyone." Wil forced himself to step away.

"I think I might like you, Mr Haines."

"Aah." Was Rhys flirting with him?

Surely not.

"Why does that sound like a threat?" he asked.

Rhys gave a breathy chuckle, and his dark lashes swept low. He looked abashed, but that couldn't be right. "I walked right into that one, didn't I?"

"I think it was me that ran into you." And, despite his embarrassment, Wil itched to do it again. To run his hands up Rhys' wide chest. Slide his fingers over Rhys' warm shoulders. Comb his fingers up through Rhys' inky curls...

"Dinner!" Yelled Evangeline from below.

Rhys flashed a half smile. "Saved by an angel."

Wil held his hands up. It probably looked like surrender, which...yes, he was guilty of inappropriate thoughts, but he hadn't actually done anything wrong.

Yet.

Clearly, he needed some alone time to go get his emotions back in check.

Wil pointed to his attic stairs, willing himself to move in that direction. But Rhys swept his arm out and bent forward in a theatrical bow. "Your servant, monsieur."

"Oh."

I like that.

What if the tables were flipped and Rhys became Wil's butler? Or his valet? His gentleman's gentleman—intimate in almost all the ways.

All thoughts of escape evaporated. Wil lifted an imaginary hat. "Thank you, Mr Buckley." He gave a gentlemanly nod and graciously descended the stairs.

Eliza Doolittle, eat your heart out.

Chapter 8

Wil

"Wine, Wil?" Rhys asked him as they entered the kitchen.

At Wil's nod, he poured a generous glass of red and placed it where Wil sat for breakfast.

Guess the tables are still turned.

"Thank you."

"Angel mentioned you watched some of my films today."

"She did?" Wil asked, stalling for time.

The woman in question set a cheesy, baked dish in the middle of the table.

"Mmm. Smells delicious. I adore your moussaka, Angel." Rhys picked up the giant serving spoon, then held out his hand. "Your plate, Wil?"

"Oh, wow. Okay." Buck House really did operate upside-down and inside-out. "Thank you, Rhys. It looks wonderful, Evangeline. Thank you."

"You're welcome." Evangeline busied herself with a bottle of fizzy water that she opened with a hiss and shared out into three cut-crystal tumblers. Then she sat on her stool and held up her glass. "Welcome to Buck House, Wil."

"Yes. Welcome." Rhys toasted with his wine.

"Thank you. It's a pleasure to be here."

"Alrighty. Enough of that. Tell me what you thought." Rhys prompted again.

"Careful what you wish for, boss." Evangeline grinned.

"Really? Why?"

She waved her fork in Wil's direction. "Tell him how many you'd seen before today."

"All of them, I hope." Rhys laughed. "Go on. I'm used to criticism. My ego can take it."

That remained to be seen. "None." Wil fessed up.

Rhys stilled, his wineglass halfway to his lip. "None?"

"Is that so unusual?"

"Ah...yes."

"We didn't have a cinema near where I grew up."

"No cinema?" Rhys shared an incredulous look with Evangeline. "I can't even imagine."

"Weird," she said. "You usually have an excellent imagination."

"Legendary," Rhys deadpanned, and Wil knew for sure they were taking the piss. "But you've seen *The Princess Bride*. You even quoted it. How can you be a cinema neophyte?"

Neophyte was a bit harsh. "The only reason I know *The Princess Bride* is because our nanny, Marcia, had a small collection of DVDs, and she always played one during nap time. I must have seen *The Princess Bride* at least a hundred times by the time I was five. It's burned into my retinas."

"Huh." Rhys' fork dangled from his fingers.

"You had a nanny?" Evangeline asked, and they both stared at him like he was an alien life form.

"Well, not me, exactly. I'm a few months older than Lord and Lady Mistlethwaite's son, David. He had nannies pretty much twenty-four seven, and we grew up together, so..." Why was he sharing personal information? It wasn't exactly pertinent to his job. "So that's how I know *The Princess Bride*, *The Sound of Music, Mary Poppins,* and *Chitty Chitty Bang Bang*. A bit later, she added *Billy Elliot* to the cycle." His favourite.

Rhys stared at him, obviously gobsmacked. "And no other movies?"

"I guess I'm just not in the habit." At their continued stare, Wil shrugged. "I know it's hard to believe, but there are other sources of entertainment."

"Let me guess. You read books. With lots and lots of words. Pictureless books. Made of paper." Rhys clutched his chest. "The poor, poor trees."

"Chiselled from stone, actually. By hand." Wil hid a smile behind his glass.

The sexy smirk was back. "Did you walk to school bare-footed too?"

"Walk? No. We rode." Wil mimed holding reins. "On ponies."

Rhys chuckled. "Wait, don't tell me...ten miles each way, rain, hail, or shine."

"Or snow." Wil took a healthy sip of the rich Merlot and rolled it around on his tongue, enjoying himself immensely. "And it was more like twelve miles. Uphill. In both directions."

Rhys raised his glass. "Cheers! To staying on ponies."

Dammit! He should've known Rhys would remember that embarrassing story.

Rhys winked. "Now, quit stalling and tell me what you thought. I'm even more interested in hearing your opinion about my work. It's a novel experience to talk to someone who's, well...out of the loop."

AKA a neophyte.

Wil cleared his throat. "I hardly think my opinion matters."

"Everyone's opinion matters. I aim to entertain. Which did you watch?"

"*Saturnine, Cave in My Heart*, and *Franky's Army*," Wil paused, searching for something positive to say. "I was moved."

"Moved." Rhys echoed, expressionless. He cocked his head. "But what did you think? Honestly? Which did you like best?"

"Um..." Wil tried to hide behind his wine. It was a large glass, but not large enough. "This is really nice. I often go for a Shiraz blend, but this Merlot complements the moussaka wonderfully."

"You didn't like them." Rhys interpreted accurately. He didn't look angry, but what did Wil know? It wasn't as though he was fully accustomed to Rhys' temperament.

Not yet.

"The wine?" Wil tried to divert the conversation one last time. "No. I said—"

"My films. Be honest now. You didn't like them, did you?"

"No! I didn't say that."

"Your reluctance to answer the question speaks volumes."

"Well…" Wil stalled. How could he answer both honestly *and* politely?

"Would you watch them again?"

"Ah…"

"I'm going to interpret that's a no."

"I'm sure they're brilliant. Just, maybe, they don't suit my taste. Art is subjective. Not everyone likes everything. Life would be boring if they did. Right?" He rushed on. "But I haven't seen all of them yet. I'll probably love the others. Maybe…if they're not quite so…"

"So what?"

Wil wracked his mind for the right word. "Dour."

Dour? Jesus, Wil. Time to shut up now.

He half expected to be banished for causing offense, but Rhys' smile only grew at Wil's scathing assessment. "Tell me why you like *The Princess Bride.*"

"I don't know." Wil shifted in his seat, wishing for a time machine, but Rhys' attention wasn't letting up. He had to give an honest answer. What had he loved about it? "Action. Adventure. True love. I liked that it's full of wonder. It's a world where anything can happen. But it all still makes sense, you know? Inside the movie. Not outside. Not here." *The Princess Bride* would never be his reality. His career was about providing order and ease. If action and adventure erupted in Wil's life, it meant he was doing something wrong. As for true love…

Wil pushed his dinner around on his plate, no longer hungry.

Rhys stared at him for an uncomfortably long time. Long enough for Wil to wonder if he really was about to get thrown out on his arse. Giving up, he put down his knife and fork, lining them up perfectly parallel on his plate. He'd apologise and be on his way. "I'm sorry. Rhys, I—"

Rhys scraped back his chair, the sound gunshot loud on the flagstone floor. "Bring out the big guns, Angel. We're in need of popcorn." He motioned to Wil. "Come on."

Too well trained not to do as he was bidden, Wil was on his feet in a nano-second. "Where are we going?"

"Not far." Rhys refilled both of their wine glasses to well above the polite level, as determined by the best sommeliers in the land, and made for the main hall. "Bring your glass, Wil."

Five minutes later, the lights in the media room were low, Wil had stretched out on the same cinema chair he'd moulded his arse to all day, and Evangeline had delivered a giant bowl of buttery popcorn into his lap.

"Remember, Wil, this viewing is strictly confidential. If the media learns anything about what you're about to watch, Jacob will run after you with a pitchfork," said Rhys.

"Ominous," Wil joked, because the warning was unnecessary. He'd already agreed not to disclose privileged information. The fact that Rhys was sharing was cause for pride, not disquiet. It showed Rhys trusted him, and Wil burned with curiosity. "What are we watching?"

"This is my current baby. I call it *Pirates: The Musical.*"

Pirates? "Seriously?"

"You're going to love it." Rhys fussed around with his laptop, connecting via Bluetooth to the tv, then he tapped a key and scooted over to sit in the chair beside Wil.

The chairs were generous, with a wide armrest between them, but Wil couldn't help shifting in his seat at their proximity. He was one hundred percent glad for the strategically placed bowl of popcorn in his lap.

"Shush," Rhys said, even though Wil hadn't said a thing. "Watch."

The familiar Buckle Up Productions logo flickered across the screen, then the film opened with a moonlit, underwater scene of tangled ships' rigging, bare legs madly treading water, and cannon balls plummeting into the dark depths with air bubbles like comet tails rushing behind.

The sound was rough. The cast sang sea-shanties with mixed degrees of talent. Half the scenes still had green-screen backgrounds awaiting digital effects. And the editing was patchy. But it didn't matter. Scene after scene, the raw energy of the adventure grabbed Wil and wouldn't let go. Even his acute awareness of Rhys slid into the background.

Two hours later, the screen flared with bright white light, then died to black, leaving a ghostly rectangle of latent light, and Wil used his imagination to insert the flow of credits scrolling by. Top billing going to Rhys Buckley—creator, director, mad-hatter.

"Well?" Rhys was leaning toward him, his elbow dug into their joint armrest.

Wil hummed and tried to play it cool. "It was alright."

"Just alright, eh?"

"Well, the whole thing's a hot mess, but..." Wil cleared his throat, embarrassed by how effusive he wanted to be.

"But what?" Rhys asked, leaning closer. "What did you think?"

A good butler was calm and composed. They did not descend into rabid fandom. But he couldn't hold back anymore. "I think...I think I've just been schooled in film-making."

Rhys exhaled in a great gust and his cock-sure grin bloomed, catching and holding every tiny scrap of light in the darkness. "Phew!" He swiped his hand across his forehead. "Thank God for that. For a minute, there I thought I might have to start all over again. New career. New life. Do you think I'd make a good undertaker? Actually, don't answer that. Given the way you feel about my other films, you'd probably encourage the move."

"Don't lose heart." Wil patted Rhys' hand. "Everyone goes through an apprenticeship phase. It's just taken you longer than most to get to the good stuff."

"Does that mean you think I'm ready to go out into the big, bad world? Try to make a name for myself?"

"Maybe." Wil paused for effect. "So long as you don't believe all the hype."

"Deal." Rhys offered his hand to shake. Sandpaper rough and popcorn warm. "Though with you around, Wil, I don't think that'll be possible. You cut me to the quick."

"It's all about not letting the world give you an enormous head," he teased.

Rhys' warm grip tightened. "Believe me, Wil. The world out there isn't to blame for that. Not tonight."

It wasn't till Wil got halfway up his attic stairs that he replayed Rhys' exact words and a whole new wave of heat rolled over him.

Fuck! I'm toast.

Chapter 9

Wil

Turned out the glory of *Pirates: The Musical* had given Wil a false sense of optimism.

Another day ensconced in the media room, watching the rest of Rhys' filmography, and Wil was feeling the hours like torture

"Please, please, please." Let it be over. He stretched his arms above his head and felt the satisfying pop of muscle and bone. At the rate he was going, he'd need both a physiotherapist *and* a psychologist to cope with spending another day in Rhys' world. Okay, that was maybe being a tad over-dramatic, but would it kill Rhys to get his actors to smile a little?

My Majesty was dreadful. He could practically feel the seedy grit of London's streets in the 90s. It made him feel like he needed an antiseptic shower and an empathetic hug. In that order.

On the other hand, *Barrow*, a thriller set in Scotland's remote northwest, was hauntingly beautiful. At least, the sweeping opening was. Wil found it impossible to get past the first scene where a victim's body was posed like a starfish, their crimson blood spattered across the inside shell of an egg-white satellite dish. If it got more or less grisly after that, Wil didn't know, since he 'watched' it from behind the palm of his hand.

"You hungry?" Evangeline asked from the doorway, making Wil leap.

He did his best to hide his surprise by climbing out of his chair and reaching for the tray of tea and sandwiches in her hands. "You are an angel. Let me get that for you."

"Thanks, Wil. Oh, I love *Barrow*. Reminds me of family holidays."

"Seriously?"

"Minus the murder and mayhem, of course. How many films have you got to go?"

Wil groaned. "One more."

"You can do it. Let me know if you need anything else." She escaped, and Wil did his best to dive back into the movie. It didn't matter that *Barrow* was a visual masterpiece, he'd lost the plot long ago.

"It's just not my cup of tea," he practiced. Surely Rhys wouldn't be offended by that. Would he?

Hell Bent on Heaven also seemed promising from the opening. The smoulderingly gorgeous, space-faring hero reminded him a little of Rhys. They shared the same sharp bone structure and mop of black curls. The only major difference was the snake-skin patch the hero wore over one eye. Then, just as Wil relaxed into it, the film descended into a nightmare of frenetic survival against a grotesque alien insect swarm, and Wil knew he'd be checking under his bed for cockroaches that night.

Did he really need to know every scene of every Rhys Buckley movie like the back of his hand in order to do his job effectively? Surely a working knowledge would do.

On the plus side, it gave him an excellent theme idea for the Autumn dinner party Jacob had tasked him to organise. So, while aliens continued to streak across the screen, chasing after the imperilled hero, Wil pulled out his notebook, opened to a fresh page, and wrote the word "Celestial" at the top. The word prompted a visual feast, including myths and legends, gods and goddesses, navigation and creation—to name just a few ideas that sparked in Wil's mind.

Depending on who Rhys wanted to invite, Wil could see some creative types showing up dressed as planets or stars, galaxies, or black holes. That, or they'd throw on a sheet and declare themselves a god or goddess. Wil closed his eyes and imagined showing up as Thor, having travelled across the universe via the Bifrost. Rhys would easily pass as Loki. Then they could be brothers...

Brothers? No. Never that.

About as good as he could do was plop one of Evangeline's copper saucepans on his head, wrap a silver belt around his waist, and call himself Orion. If he was a guest, that was. But he wasn't a guest. He was the butler. He needed to maintain a dignified distance.

And what about Rhys? From what Wil had seen, the man's imagination was without limit. If not Loki, who or what would he dress as? Would he gravitate to being a hero or an anti-hero? Human or alien?

Wil flicked his attention back to the screen, where the fate of the celluloid humans seemed sealed in the realms of hell. Grappling with his faltering spaceship, and a hedonistic posse of unlikely companions, the one-eyed hero charged through alien-riddled space. All seemed lost when, dark against the zillion pinpricks of galaxies in the universe, a wormhole coalesced, inky black.

A pathway out.

The hero's desperate hope for survival pulled Wil along. Heart strung tight, he shoved the foot rest back under the plush leather seat and sat forward, willing him on. "Escape! Escape! Go, go, go!"

Cut to the hero's visage, wide-eyed in horror...or maybe desperation, Wil wasn't sure.

Zoom in on the hero's eye. Iris. Pupil. Filling the screen. Reflecting the hero's singular view. The deep darkness of a black hole closing in.

Wil teetered on the edge of his seat. Racing heart turned feral.

Then, in the middle of the inky black, a single speck of starlight appeared.

A mournful note broke the silence...swelled into a chord.

The chord built to a wild crescendo...morphed into a symphony.

One star streaming warp speed split the darkness...fractured into more.

And the hero's singular, one-eyed view expanded into fractals of brilliant starlight.

Then, *WHOOMPH!*

Wil gasped at the sudden absence of sight and sound.

Pitch black.

Silence.

Sensory deprivation.

Wil slapped a shaky hand over the frantic beat of his heart. "Oh. My. God."

"It gets you, doesn't it?"

"Holy shit!" Heart out of his chest, he spun around to see Evangeline leaning in the doorway. Casual as could be.

"Gotcha!" She laughed.

"Jesus. I can't believe he sucked me in. What happened? Did the guy blink? Or, what?"

"Nobody knows." Evangeline shrugged. "Except maybe Rhys. Doesn't it make you want to shake him and kiss him all at the same time?"

"Hell, yes!" Shit. "I mean. Of course not. Shake, yes. Kiss, no." Hell no. Not at all.

Evangeline nodded, as though she understood exactly what his ramblings meant. Which was a good thing—at least one of them was clued in.

"Listen, I'm heading off early for the day," she said. "I've left a pot of mushroom soup in the fridge. Just sit it on the warm side of the Aga for a half hour before you and Rhys are ready to eat. There's a fresh sourdough loaf under the tea towel."

"Thanks Evangeline, sounds delicious. Are there any deliveries I still need to deal with?"

"A couple of packages, and there's a pile of letters on Jacob's desk. Nothing's marked urgent, but best check yourself. Rhys hates things being left till later. 'Why do tomorrow what you can do today', he always says." She rolled her eyes.

"Hmm." Wil evaded answering. Rhys' work ethic sounded about right to him. "Thanks for stepping in for me today, Evangeline. I promise to be up and butling tomorrow."

"Butling!" She snorted. "Anyway, I best get on. Nick wants to check out a new baby store in Reading. He's a toucher. Which explains this little possum, if you know what I mean." She laughed and stroked her belly. "But he can't buy anything without feeling it first. Drives me nuts."

"Thanks Evangeline. Take care on the road. It was frosty this morning."

"Thanks, Dad," she scoffed, and waved goodbye.

Wil heard the front door clunk shut, and was suddenly hyper-aware that he was alone in the house with his boss.

The push-pull between them was a problem Wil didn't know how to solve. Other than to ignore it and get to work.

Sure. No problem, Haines.

"Shut up, inner-sarcasm."

And for your next trick?

Grr…

Luckily, there were other things he could solve. Other things he could control.

Focus on your training, Wil. He switched off the media system and stood up to stretch. It did little to realign his psyche, but his spine popped with approval.

He crossed the hall and entered the kitchen. "A cup of tea is definitely in order."

"What are you trying to solve?"

"Agh! Don't do that!" What was it with the Buck House inhabitants always sneaking up on him?

Rhys leaned against the kitchen island, dressed head to toe in navy camo. The sun streamed in through the window behind him, creating angel fire around his form. He looked to Wil like a wet dream.

"Running away to the Royal Marines, are we?" The possibility was unlikely, but it would solve one of his problems—hard to lust after your boss when they're an ocean away.

"You like?" Rhys asked.

Answer that without blushing, I dare you.

"Lex gave me this outfit for my birthday. She's forever teasing me about my appalling navigation skills. Says I'd probably lose myself if I wore army camouflage in the jungle gym. But the navy colours take care of that problem. It's a bit much, in my humble opinion."

Or not so humble. "So, you're not running away?"

Rhys laughed. "Don't sound so disappointed!"

"No. I'm not—" *Fuck.* Wil zipped his mouth shut and diverted his attention to the kettle. With any luck, a restorative cup of tea would fix his acute case of foot-in-mouth disease.

"It's alright. I forgive you. Though at this rate, you're going to give me a complex. First, you reject my films. Now, you reject my company?" He hung his head low. "What does a poor guy need to do to win your approval?"

"Do you need it?"

"There's that sass I like. You're not getting rid of me yet, though. Just thought I'd get some exercise in today."

Hence the mouth-watering physique.

Rhys patted his non-existent pot belly. "The camera puts on twenty pounds."

"I hardly think you have anything to worry about. Besides, don't you work behind the camera?"

"That never stopped the tabloids. But thanks. Nice to know my butler appreciates my physique." He winked. "By the way, feel free to use it as a stress-reliever."

Hells, yes.

"I mean the jungle gym. Not...not me." Rhys stumbled over his words. "Not my body. Even though...well...yeah..."

Was it his imagination, or had Rhys' cheeks turned pink?

Wil straightened up. Was Rhys affected by their close proximity, too? Maybe he wasn't the only one feeling befuddled every time he was in his boss' orbit. And it would only get worse, given how close they'd have to work together. Not just in Buck House, but on the road, too. Jacob had made it pretty clear that the focus of his job wasn't the house itself. It was the master of the house. Wherever Rhys went, he'd go, too.

"An intriguing idea." One he would never, ever, follow through on. Given Wil's extreme clumsiness, he'd be face first in the freezing cold creek within seconds. "Assign me a stunt-double, and I'm in."

"Like that, is it?" Rhys huffed a low chuckle and sidled up beside Wil to drop his used mug into the kitchen sink. Close enough for Wil to feel the zing of awareness. "Syd would love it if you gave the gym a go. He's forever inviting around guinea pigs. Just don't kill yourself. It's a long way from Buck House to the emergency room."

The zing didn't fray a single bit as Rhys stepped away to the back door. He wrapped a scarf around his neck and thumbed open the brass latch. "I'll be back in a few hours for dinner," he promised and headed off toward his treehouse.

Wil shivered against the fresh chill, but didn't budge from the kitchen window, staring at Rhys' tapered back till he disappeared from view.

"Get to work, Wil." He reminded himself. He placed his dirty mug next to Rhys' in the farmhouse sink, connected his phone to the Bluetooth speaker in the office, and pressed play on his favourite productivity mood music. The perfect atmosphere to tackle his already extensive to-do list.

With only a few short weeks to organise the dinner party, the pressure to perform was immense. It had to be unforgettable. No loose ends. Nothing left to chance.

Chapter 10

Wil

E vangeline had certainly been busy while he'd sequestered himself away in Rhys' movie-worlds. As evidenced by the pile of post that teetered on the edge of Jacob's...no, *his* desk, and the two larger packages piled by the wall.

Wil separated out the envelopes marked 'confidential' and put them aside for Rhys to review privately, then ripped open the others. Most turned out to junk mail mixed in with em-bossed invitations to red-carpet events. Then he turned his attention to the cluster of smaller packages originating from the same London address. Inside were hard-drives labelled with non-consecutive numbers in silver marker.

Wil added "coordinate couriers for better efficiency" to his to-do list and put the hard-drives aside to take to the editing suite in the garage studio.

The smaller of the two large packages held bubble-wrapped plastic figurines—a hammerhead shark, a giant squid, and three human characters that looked vaguely like the characters in *Pirates: The Musical*.

"Jesus." They were ugly as sin. "Hope Rhys isn't the type to shoot the messenger."

The last package was the size and shape of a pre-teen's casket, wrapped in brown paper and tied up with string. Had someone sent a macabre *The Sound of Music* present?

Wil hummed along to Julie Andrews in his head as he fiddled with the ties. Visions of raindrops and whiskers and kettles and mittens streaking through his mind.

Should he open it?

They'd addressed it to "Peter Buckley of Buck House". That was it. No town. No postcode.

The return address was even less helpful.

"C. Hook of Liverpool". Nothing else. Not even a postmark.

In fact, none of the letters or packages had standard Royal Mail postage stamps attached. Presumably, they'd all come by courier. Which meant whatever the postie had delivered was probably still in the letterbox beyond the gate.

Wil pulled out his ballooning to-do list, added "post", then decided he might as well tick that one off while he got some fresh air after being cooped up by the cold autumn rain.

The gravel crunched under his feet. Small animals scratched in the undergrowth, and birds twittered in the trees. He couldn't help feel a kinship with the stealthy creatures—securing their nests, stockpiling for winter—all without drawing undue attention.

Wil hadn't done the greatest job of going un-noticed himself. But there was time yet. He just had to get into his groove.

Wil diverted around the gate to where the fence bisected the back of the dollhouse-slash-post-box-slash-security-check-point. He hadn't brought his key to unlock the top section, which housed the motion detector and video camera, but he could access the opening of the post box without issue. He half expected it to be full, but there were only a few letters inside, and he couldn't shake a weird feeling of disappointment as he trudged back along the gravel drive with his light haul, kicking a sharp stone ahead with his toe.

Why was he so disappointed? It made no sense.

Wil catalogued his situation.

"Perfect job."

Mostly.

Kick.

"Perfectly imperfectly boss."

Definitely.

Kick.

"Perfect home."

Check.

Kick.

"Perfectly happy."

Umm.

Kick.

"Hang on."

What was he missing?

"Nothing's missing. This is you being a perfectionist."

Kick.

"Get over yourself."

Kick.

"Decide to be happy, and move on."

Kick.

"As though it's that easy."

Kick.

It is, Wil.

Kick.

Yeah right.

Kick.

The ghost of Rhys' wild hair tangled around his fingers.

Wil stopped.

What the fuck was that?

To shake off the feeling, he made fists, clenching tight. When that didn't work, he made jazz hands, stretching taught.

Nope.

The birds kept twittering, and the squirrels kept scrounging, but Wil couldn't move forward another inch.

What had tripped his mind up?

Aside from thoughts of your gloriously handsome boss?

"Uh-huh. Aside from him."

Well...

Wil couldn't think of anything.

Never mind that his future was an unknown. All he needed to do was stay on task in the here and now. Organise Buck House. Respond as needed. Be the rock.

Simple.

Newly affirmed, Wil toed off his wet shoes in the front entry, returned to Jacob's white-on-white office, fiddled with the desk chair to get the ergonomics just right, dealt with the last of the post, and flipped to the November end of his day-per-page butler's diary.

"Time to get organised."

He grabbed a ruler from the drawer and marked a vertical line down the middle. On the left side, he wrote out the household schedule. On the right, he noted his accomplishments that day, including a rating and reminder keyword for each of his boss's films. Rhys probably wouldn't appreciate his subjective opinions, but Wil had to be scrupulously honest in his butler's diary.

That was the only way.

On future dates, he added planned events and milestones to keep him on track. Then he colour-coded for priority.

Normally, organising gave Wil a sense of calm satisfaction. Instead, he felt increasingly twitchy, his heart tick-tick-ticking faster than the grandfather clock in the hall.

Huh. That was weird. He couldn't usually hear the grandfather clock all the way back in the office? Was it the acoustics? Or was it because Buck House was practically a still life when only he and Rhys were home? If it wasn't for the clockwork ticking, he'd wonder if time hadn't stopped too.

He paused the mood music and reversed his way back to the front of the grand hall to check the grandfather clock. The crank-wound clock was ticking, but not as loud or clear as he'd heard it earlier.

Huh. Even more of a puzzle.

And when he got back to the office, the sound was slightly louder.

Huh. Even weirder.

Had Jacob stashed an old-fashioned alarm clock in his desk drawers?

When that search came up barren, Wil closed his eyes, eased his breathing, and listened intently for the origin of the tick, tick, tick...

It was faint, but definitely...

There!

He opened his eyes, landing immediately on the coffin-shaped package from Liverpool.

"You are now, officially, *not* one of my favourite things."

Wil got down on his knees and placed his ear to the brown-paper package.

The tick-tick echoed through. Clear as day.

God. Please, no.

They'd trained him at the academy to respond to security risks. Told him to wear gloves even when opening letters, to scan packages with a metal detector, to treat every stranger as a threat. But that was all theoretical. It hadn't been real. Nothing he learned at the Bourneworth Academy of Household Management had prepared him for a fucking coffin at his boss' door with a ticking timebomb inside.

What the hell was he going to do?

Wil held his breath as he gingerly eased his ear away and eased to his feet, leaned to reach for his phone on the desk, then slowly backed out of the office on his socked feet.

The screech of the closing office door was like fingers on a chalkboard. He shivered, despite the toasty warmth of the kitchen.

"Please, please, please..."

Dare he make a phone call?

Could it signal a trigger and set the bomb off?

If it even was a bomb. It could be completely innocent, Wil.

Yeah, right. The thing ought to come with a big warning sign saying, "IGNORE AT YOUR PERIL." No way was Wil not treating it as a real and present danger.

Unfortunately, none of that certainty kept his heart rate steady as he pulled the back door shut and raced around the back corner of the house to the base of Rhys' tree.

"Rhys!" He hollered.

The low afternoon sun glinted on the treehouse windows. Rhys was usually up there at that time of day, but nothing moved.

"Rhys!" He tried again.

No sound emerged.

"Where the hell are you, Rhys?" Desperately, he jangled at the bell, over and over. No response came, and all he could hear in his mind was the echo of the tick, tick, tick.

Precious time raced by. Heart in his throat, Wil madly flicked through his contacts' list for Rhys' phone number, then pressed the green dial icon.

One ring, two rings... "Please, please, please pick up". As the dial tone rung a third time, Wil took off running around the house to the garage studio.

"You have dialled oh-four-two-seven-one-six-seven-two-five-nine. Please leave a message after the beep...*BEEP.*"

"Rhys, it's Wil. Please pick up. There's a situation here. There's a...well...I'm not sure, but there might be a bomb in your house. It's ticking and...I...oh, God...I don't know where you are. Please call me. I'm calling the...*BEEP*...fuck!"

At the studio door, he tapped in the security code, hauled the door open, and hollered into the darkness. "Rhys!" His high, panicked voice reverberated around the massive space, but once again, there was no response. "Where are you!?"

He re-dialled Rhys' number and suffered through the message again before finally he could speak.

BEEP.

"Rhys. It's Wil. I'm calling the police. Just, please, don't go inside the house. Buck House. Your house. Shit. Call me. Except don't, coz I'm calling the police. Fuck. This is so not happening. Why is this happening? Hope you're okay. Fuck. Gotta go. Bye."

He hung up and dialled 999.

"Hello. Emergency services officer. Which service do you require? Fire, police, or ambulance?

"Police! Police! Police!"

Calm the fuck down, Haines. He coached himself. *It's just an itty-bitty bomb.*

Maybe.

What if it's a big one?

You know nothing about bombs.

But what if it is?

Doubt swam in Wil's mind. How was he supposed to be the rock of Buck House, when he fell apart at the slightest hint of a threat?

He pushed at his swirling thoughts. Tamped down his fear. No matter the threat to Buck House, his priority was Rhys.

Always Rhys.

Find him. Make sure he's safe.

"Connecting you now." The emergency services officer interrupted his manic thoughts.

A few clicks and a dial tone rang before another woman picked up. "Hello. Police."

"Help! There's a bomb. It's ticking. What do I do? I need help."

Jesus, Wil. Calm...the fuck...down.

"Slow down. Tell me your name and where you are."

"Buck House. I'm Wil Haines. I'm the butler. I'm only new and I don't know..."

"Where is Buck House?" The clack of computer keys was audible through the line. "What's your town, street name, house number? Are there any distinctive features?"

Wil struggled to unscramble his thoughts.

Focus! Be the rock.

"Umm. Between Hewstoke Woods and Cantnoor Cross. There's a sign at the junction. I don't remember what was on it. It's—"

"Buck House. I have it. Oak Tree Lane."

"Yes!" Thank God.

"And where is the device?"

"The bomb?"

"Yes."

"Inside Buck House!" Was the woman deaf? Obtuse? Have the memory of a sieve?

"Is anyone injured?"

"No. But it's ticking, and I can't find my boss." His heart tripped. All he could think of was Rhys. Where the hell was he?

"Stay on the line, please."

The sound of his own sharp breaths overwhelmed everything.

"Wil Haines?" She was back, thank God.

"Yes. It's me."

"Where are you now? Are you in immediate danger?" The woman asked, her voice tinged with authority.

"I don't know." Wil shivered in his thin shirtsleeves. "I'm outside."

"Is the device inside or outside?"

"It's in the house. In the off...office." He couldn't help stuttering.

"Okay. Get as far away as you can. Is there anyone else in the house or the immediate surrounds?"

"Yes. Maybe. Oh, God. Rhys. I don't know where Rhys is. He was home. But now I can't find him. I tried to call him, but he's not answering."

"Rhys Buckley?"

"Yes." How did the woman know? Was Rhys really that famous?

"Okay, Wil. Listen to me carefully. Go to the security gate and wait there for the police and the explosive ordnance disposal unit. You will need to let them through the gate when they arrive. Can you do that?"

"Of course." He raced down the pebbled driveway, still in his socked feet. "Ouch!"

Is this what it feels like to walk on coals?

"Are you okay?"

"I'm fine." He winced. "I just don't have any shoes on."

"The police are almost there. Can you get to the gate safely?"

"Of course." He'd do his duty. No matter what.

Where was Rhys?

"Rhys!" he hollered.

"Is Mr Buckley nearby?"

"No. I don't know where he is."

"Okay. Hang on, Wil. You're doing great."

"Great. Sure. Spectacular." What hope did he have of being the rock when his world felt like quicksand?

Chapter 11

Rhys

R hys' heart hammered and his lungs heaved as he rolled over the final rope obstacle and landed on his arse in the cold leaf-litter and mud. Every muscle protested as he pressed the stop button on his smart watch. Thirty-seven minutes, sixteen seconds. A personal best. "Yes! Take that, Sydney Buckley!" His breath streamed out in visible clouds.

Somewhere in the vicinity, another police siren wailed, interrupting his celebration. They'd been echoing up the steep sides of the valley for at least ten minutes. The bloody noise had scared off the wildlife, destroyed the peace of the woods, and almost made him break his stride.

Almost.

When he latched onto a target, very little could sway Rhys from his goal.

Every muscle protested as he forced himself up to stand on wobbly legs, and he made a half-arsed effort to wipe off the muddy muck that clung to his blue camos. He slipped and slid on the steep leaf-strewn path up to the garden flat surrounding his home. When he got there, though, the scene wasn't at all what he expected.

"What the...?"

His home looked like something straight out of a Hollywood B movie. The place was eerily silent, but police swarmed around his house, and there were so many flashy blue lights they lit up the low-lying clouds.

"Hey!" A half-dozen officers stood in a huddle near the door to the kitchen, wearing reflective safety glasses and enough armour to look like extras from a bad *RoboCop* reboot. At his shout, their heads all swivelled his way. Then, in synchrony, they turned back to their task.

Creepy.

One of them gave a bellowing order, two rushed to take positions on either side of the kitchen door, a third raised a full-body shield, and a fourth drew back a battering ram.

"Hey!" Rhys raced forward across the rain-slick grass. "What the hell are you doing?" Nobody attacked Buck House. Not on his watch.

"Rhys! Stop!"

"Wil?"

Rhys swerved toward his butler's voice, but his trainers lost their grip and he couldn't stop the momentum of his initial trajectory. One leg slid forward, the other anchored behind, and he heard the telltale sound of fabric ripping as he slid into an involuntary split. "Fuck!"

That's gonna hurt.

"Wil," he ground out. His butler sure had some explaining to do.

Come to think of it, where was Wil? That had been his voice Rhys heard, for sure.

"Mr Buckley!" A young female officer, clutching a police bowler hat tight to her head, rose from behind the dry-stone garden wall.

Wil popped up beside her. "Rhys! There's a bo—agh!" The officer shoved at Wil's shoulder, forcing him to the ground. "Hey!"

"Get away from the house!" The officer shouted, motioning wildly.

"Run, Rhys!" Wil yelled from behind the wall. "There's a bomb!"

A bomb?

That got him running, but the wet grass was slick as ice.

"Quick!" cried the officer. "We need you a safe distance from the blast radius."

Blast radius?

Had he bumped his head and landed in one of his own movies?

He searched the grey skies.

No alien spaceships.

Thank God for that.

"Move your arse, Rhys!" Wil screamed. His fingertips were white where he gripped a rock on the top of the wall.

Rhys slipped and slid across the vast expanse in as straight a line as he could manage.

Why was he taking orders from his butler? He was the boss. Not the employee. It was his job to make demands. He rounded the dry-stone wall and ducked down beside Wil. "What in the seven flames of hell is going on here?"

Wil flinched at Rhys' harsh tone, but he kept eye-contact. Rhys would give him that. "Buck House is the target," Wil said.

"We don't know that," the officer said.

Wil shoved her hand from his shoulder, his spine rigid. "I saw it myself, Rhys. They sent it to—"

"We don't know anything yet."

Wil glared at her. "Well, I sure hope you bloody well know something. We're not sniffing roses here, Gertrude."

"My name's not Gertrude. It's Constable Frazer," she said, pointing to the name badge on her uniform.

"That's not the point." Wil huffed.

"What *is* the point?"

"The point is there's a bloody bomb in the bloody house and nobody's gone in to deactivate the bloody thing. That's what."

Jesus. Is it weird that I think my butler is sexy fierce?

Probably.

"Clear!" came a booming voice.

Rhys jumped up like a jackrabbit.

"Get down!" Wil leaped at him. Pushed him down.

"Oof!" He grunted, sandwiched between the soggy ground and Wil's lanky body. It wasn't the worst place to be, but still...what the fuck was going on?

"Shh!" Wil shushed him, even though he'd not said a thing, and Rhys' senses filled with Wil's quick breaths, and the very familiar aroma of slightly sweet, slightly salty popcorn.

It shouldn't have been alluring.

He was lying on damp, rocky ground, with his butler on top of him. He had an eight-inch hole in his pants that he did *not* intend to put to good use. And, apparently, a bomb was about to blow up his precious home.

Not a good time to for his dick to throw a semi into the mix.

"Get off me, you oaf." Rhys tried, unsuccessfully, to elbow Wil's gut. "I don't—"

"Shh!" Wil slapped a hand across his mouth, too quick for Rhys to close it. The sweet salt was stronger there. He could taste it on Wil's palm.

Oh, God. Not peachy. Not peachy at all.

They'd landed beyond the safety of the stone wall in such a way that they both had a rabbit's-eye view on the kitchen door where the RoboCop with the shield was reaching out to the brass door latch, his hand in a fucking gauntlet for a glove.

It was like some kind of *Highlander*-meets-*Hot Fuzz* montage.

Gospel truth.

"Look." Wil jerked his chin at Buck House, making his bristles abrade against Rhys' dense beard, like fingers stroking velvet the wrong way—so wrong and yet so very right.

He shuddered.

"Are you cold?" Wil whispered into his ear.

"No." *Far from it.* Though some parts of him were chilled to the bone.

Rhys would be the first to admit that he didn't know what to do with a butler, but would it be so very wrong of him to ask Wil to slide down behind him and warm up his cold arse cheeks?

Pretty please?

He wriggled a bit.

There were accidents...and then there was providence.

Before he could gussy up the courage to ask, movement happened at the kitchen door.

Everyone, even the birds, were so dead silent that Rhys could hear the click of the door latch and the high C screech as it swung inward, then...

Nothing.

Constable Frazer put a finger to her ear, and her expression went distant. Rhys guessed she was listening through an earpiece. When her gaze cleared, she turned to face the flashy lights in his driveway. Rhys followed her line of sight and noticed a new truck had joined the party. Taller than the other police vehicles, he could easily make out the shouty words: *EXPLOSIVE ORDNANCE DISPOSAL UNIT.*

Suddenly, it was all far too real. He pushed at Wil, detangling enough to get his feet underneath his arse and squat eye-height to the top of the dry-stone wall. "What in the actual fuck is going on, Constable Frazer?"

"Your butler received a suspicious package."

Wil piped up. "It was Evangeline, actually. She was answering the door for me. I didn't see who delivered it."

"Okay." It wasn't the first time he'd received an odd gift from one of his fans. "What was it?"

"A bomb."

"We don't know that." She glared at Wil.

"It was ticking," Wil insisted, his voice edged with tension.

"Ticking?"

"Yes, *ticking*."

Rhys turned to the constable. "Are you telling me some crazy fan sent me a bomb?"

"We cannot be sure it's a bomb yet, Mr Buckley. Not until the team investigates. But your butler was correct to be suspicious. As a public figure, you're a typical soft target."

Soft? My arse.

"Mr Buckley isn't a typical anything," Wil protested.

He put a stilling hand to Wil's forearm. "Stand down, soldier."

"This is serious, Mr Buckley," she said.

"Some of my fans might border on obsessive, but nobody's ever tried to hurt me. I make movies, for God's sake. This is kind of overkill, don't you think?" He'd directed to question to Constable Frazer, but it was Wil that answered.

"You're wrong."

"Hey! You're supposed to be on my side."

"I am on your side. That's why I called the police. And that's why I'm telling you the truth. I've heard way too many horror stories on Plain Jane about celebrities getting caught up with obsessive types."

"They're fans. Not crazy."

"Says you."

"Yeah. Says me. And I'm the boss." *So there!*

"Gentlemen." Constable Frazer broke through their dispute and pointed at the kitchen door where a robot crept excruciatingly slowly up the shallow step, through the kitchen door, and disappeared into Buck House.

Then, a horrifying memory of the Maxwell School kidnapper surfaced, and any concern for his own safety went completely out the window. "Syd and Lex!"

"Sir. Please calm down."

"Calm down? How can I possibly calm down when my kids could be in danger?" His mind reeled with thoughts of murder.

He grabbed the constable's sleeve. "They're the softest targets. And Miriam. I have to call them." Rhys grabbed instinctively for the back pocket of his camo trousers.

Nothing.

Where's my phone?

What fucking shithouse timing he had to leave it on the charger by his bed.

Timing! Of course!

"Never mind," he muttered while, heart racing, he swiped at his smart watch, scrambling through all the bells and whistles for the call feature. But he couldn't get his fucking hands to work. They felt twice their usual size.

"Calm down, Rhys." Wil stilled his jittering hand for a bare half second. "Panicking won't help."

Right. He was right. "I know."

Focus, Buckley.

"Are they in school right now?" asked Constable Frazer.

"Yes. The Maxwell School. East of Oxford."

Syd and Lex might be soft targets—the bullseye of his heart—but they were smart kids. He'd taught them not to trust strangers. To be prepared. Problem was, their school was a safe zone. Neither would be primed to act in self-defence. Not there.

The constable relayed the information through her radio. "We'll send officers to make sure they're okay, but we have no cause to think they're in danger."

Wil paled. He pulled his own phone from his jeans pocket. "I think I saved the school's direct number. Just in case, you know?"

"Thank God." Rhys grabbed it from Wil. "I'm calling Lex."

Constable Frazer flattened her hand over the phone's screen. Not touching. Just obstructing. "And what will you tell her, Mr Buckley?"

"What do you think, officer? I'm going to make sure my kids are safe."

"Rhys, maybe..." Wil started.

"What?" His voice was sharp. Probably too sharp, but he didn't give a shit. This was serious. He wasn't fucking around.

"I'm scared for them, too. But if you go in all guns blazing, they're going to be terrified. Do you want that?"

The 'no' lodged in his throat. Did Wil really think he wanted to scare his kids? "I'm not going to tell them a bomb is about to blow up their home."

Wil stared at him. Unnaturally calm. "I know you just want to hear their voices. But right now, the school is better equipped to locate Syd and Lex and to make sure they're okay."

Rhys looked down at the phone in the vice grip of his hand. Thumb poised to press 'call'. Was Wil right?

God! What if he made the wrong decision?

"Think of it like fitting your own oxygen mask in a plane," Wil said. "You can't protect them if you don't first protect yourself."

"The robot is already in there gathering information." Constable Frazer weighted in. "When we know something concrete, then we can act."

"Rhys. Lex and Syd aren't here." Wil pointed out. "I heard a ticking and panicked. But, really, this could all be nothing."

"You wouldn't've called the police if you thought that." Although Wil might have a point. If Rhys tried to talk to his niece or nephew right then, he'd lose it for sure.

Wil took the phone from Rhys' numb hands and spun again through his contact list for *The Maxwell School*.

"Here." Wil showed the officer the details.

"I can't just sit here. I have to do something." At the rate Rhys was going, he'd jitter out of his own skin.

He reached for Wil's hand and gave it a squeeze. It was probably odd, but Rhys didn't care. The man's touch felt good.

Necessary.

"How'd you get so wise?"

"Comes with the butler DNA." Wil flashed a half smile, then touched the call and speaker icons so they could all hear.

The ringtone jangled, grating Rhys' nerves.

"What do we actually know?" Wil asked the constable in a strangled voice. It was the question Rhys would have asked at the first hint of trouble, if he'd had his wits about him.

"Yes." Rhys leaped in. "What do you know?"

"Very little, so far. When Wil heard the package ticking, it was prudent for him to contact us. Now, we just have to wait for the robot to do its job."

"A package from—"

"The Maxwell School," said the school secretary. "Please hold."

"Wait, Mrs Westram! This is urgent. Don't put me on hold," Rhys spoke so fast it was a wonder he didn't trip over his own tongue.

"Rhys Buckley?"

Too many times, he'd heard that strident voice on his visits to the principal's office during his school years. It wouldn't make him back down, though. Not this time. "Yes. It's me. I need to speak to Principal Lewis. Immediately."

"He's on a call with the police now. Does this have something to do with you? What on earth is going on, Mr Buckley?" Her words were uncannily close to his own thoughts. It was scary. But he didn't have time to explain anything.

"I'm sorry, Mrs Westram." So much for not backing down. "I don't mean to be impertinent, but—"

"Hold, please." Tinny elevator music filled the air.

"Fuck!" He looked straight at Wil. "This feels like a gotcha movie. Are you sure we're not being filmed right now?"

Wil groaned. "Not one of your films, I hope."

"Why not?"

"Because they're dark as Hades. Everything always goes badly."

Rhys felt a full-body jerk.

I was the bald-faced truth, but, Jesus, what a time to point it out.

"Sorry, Rhys. I'm just so...sorry. You put your trust in me, and I'm just...God. I'm inept."

"Don't do that." Wil had been spitting fire minutes ago, and Rhys wanted it...needed it back. "You were only trying to protect me and mine." He couldn't fault Wil for that. "It's me that's sorry for jumping down your throat. Come on, Wil. Where's that sass I like? You're okay. I'm okay. The kids will be okay. Right, Constable Frazer?"

"Ah..." Her gaze was far away.

"*Right*, Constable Frazer?"

Rhys wasn't an idiot. He knew the woman couldn't confirm anything, but that didn't stop the desperate desire to hear good news...or the longing to make Wil feel better.

Which was just plain weird. Since when was it his job to take care of his butler? Talk about life flipping inside out and upside down.

The constable stiffened, and she put a finger to her ear. Rhys wanted to interrogate her, but she held her hand up to him while she listened intently.

"Addressed to a Peter Buckley? Please confirm. Over."

That got his attention, and Rhys suddenly had an awful, and wonderful, thought. "Wait. Did you say it was addressed to Peter Buckley?"

"Yes." Wil leaped in before she could answer. "I figured he was a relative."

"Oh, my God." If only Wil had found him first. They could have avoided all the drama. The worry. Still, it paid to be sure.

He tightened his grip on Wil's hand. "Who sent it?"

"I don't know. Someone in Liverpool. I didn't recognise the name."

"Who was the sender?" She listened again. "C. Hook. Please confirm."

C. Hook? Oh, hell. Miriam wouldn't have. Rhys almost laughed at how ludicrous the whole circus was, only none of it was funny. He shoved his free hand into the hair at his temple and tugged. "Call off the dogs, Constable."

"Why?" Wil grabbed his wrist. "Who's this C. Hook, Rhys?"

Constable Frazer held up a quieting finger. Seconds later, she gave him the nod. "Correct."

"Ah, fuck." What a mess.

"Do you know those people?" She asked.

"Yeah. I know them." He couldn't help but chuckle as he took in the shit show they'd made of his house. "Bloody hell, this'll go down as a true Buckley legend."

"Who was it?" Wil asked, but Rhys couldn't answer.

The more he thought about it, the more obvious the joke was. His chuckle became a full-throated laugh.

"This isn't funny, Rhys!" Wil grabbed his hand. "Get down!"

Rhys placed the phone on the top of the wall where they would all still be able to hear when Mrs Westram ever deigned to take him off hold. Then he hauled the reluctant Wil up and wrapped him up in a celebratory bear hug.

"Rhys! Let me go. What is wrong with you?" Wil pushed at his chest, but Rhys didn't let go.

God, it felt good.

"Rhys Buckley. If you get me killed, I will never forgive you."

"Not going to get you killed. Everything's okay. I promise."

"That's reassuring. Not."

There'd been no actual risk, but Wil hadn't known that. His instinct had been to protect. He'd come out in the freezing cold, with no coat, and no shoes, and his only thought had been for Rhys and for Buck House.

"Thank you," Rhys whispered into his ear, then pulled back enough to see Wil's expression. He couldn't contain his grin. "I can't believe she actually did it."

"She? Who? Did what? Stop smiling like a dolt and tell me what you know before I strangle you."

"Blood-thirsty soul! I never knew you had it in you."

"Rhys," he growled. "This is so not funny."

"It is, actually." He chuckled into Wil's hair. It smelled awfully nice.

The elevator music stopped. "Rhys? Hello? Mrs Westram, I thought you said Rhys Buckley was on this line?"

"I'm here, Robert," Rhys called out, still unable to contain the laughter that came with his relief.

"Who's that?" asked Wil.

"Robert Lewis. Principal at The Maxwell School."

"Rhys? What have you done now? The police just called with a cryptic story about a bomb. Are you okay? Why are you laughing? Mrs Westram, he's laughing."

The secretary picked up on a third line. "Mr Buckley. Please enlighten us about the situation. And do remember the danger of crying wolf."

"Yes, ma'am." He finally swallowed his laughter. Nothing like a rebuke from Mrs Westram to set him straight. She'd been scary back in the nineties, when he and Miriam had boarded year-round. Nearly two decades later, the woman was only slightly less terrifying.

"Rhys. What on earth is going on down there?" Robert asked.

"Hello Robert. My butler and the police are all here, and they want the same information. You're on speaker."

"A butler? You? Now I know you're joking."

Mrs Westram hmm'd her equal disbelief. "Campus security is escorting Alexandra and Sydney from their classes. What are we to tell them, Mr Buckley? You will not frighten those dear, sweet children. Do you hear me?"

That put Rhys' back up. "My only concern is for their safety." Scaring Syd and Lex was the last thing he'd ever want to do.

"You were laughing, Mr Buckley."

"Yes, I'm sorry Mrs Westram. That must have sounded odd, but new information has come to light that proves there's no threat."

"Proof? What proof?" Wil's voice rose, his colour high.

"I'm glad to hear that, Mr Buckley."

"Thank you, Mrs Westram."

"Excuse me," Constable Frazer interrupted, "What new information are you referring to, Mr Buckley?"

"My middle name is Peter."

"Peter!" Wil jumped in. "So, I was right. They really did send the bomb to you."

"No...well, yes, they sent the package to me. But no, there's no way it's a bomb." Two sets of eyes and the blinking phone stared expectantly back at him. "I don't know what it is, or why it's ticking, but it's not a bomb. Of that, I'm certain. It's from my sister, and she'd never hurt me or Buck House." She may have mothered Syd and Lex from a distance, but she'd never do anything to hurt her children. "Doesn't Peter and C. Hook ring a bell with any of you? Peter Pan and Captain Hook? It's just silly enough to be one of Miriam's jokes."

Robert groaned. "Bloody Miriam. Sounds like something she would do."

"Right?" At least someone got it. "Unfortunately, she doesn't always think through her practical jokes."

"Send her my love, would you, Rhys? I'll do my best to take care of things at this end, but expect a call from your niece and nephew."

"Thanks Robert. Talk to you soon." He disconnected the call and turned to the constable. "Miriam is my sister. She played Tinker Bell in a Christmas pantomime last December. I'm guessing she must have stopped through Liverpool and sent me a souvenir from the production."

The constable clicked on her radio to relay the new information, and Rhys turned his attention back to Wil, who was shaking.

"God, you're frozen." He wrapped Wil in his arms and rubbed his back. "Where's your jacket? And your shoes? You didn't plan this disaster very well, did you?"

Wil huffed. "This is so unprofessional," he muttered into Rhys' shoulder.

"Don't care." Rhys muttered back. The man felt so good in his arms.

As chaos stirred around them, relief crashed down and all Rhys wanted was to curl up together—to wallow in Wil's earnest care.

Another shudder rippled through Wil's body.

Rhys tightened his hold. "You'll be lucky to get away from today without contracting pneumonia."

"There's the drama king I know and love. Uh, I mean." Wil inched away, but Rhys wasn't ready for him to go.

Give him an out, Buckley. "Don't worry," he said. "In my world, 'love' is a throwaway term. If you'd said 'like', well now, that might've had me blushing." He looked around at the ridiculous scene. Dusk was settling, the shadows growing, making the blue lights flash brighter than ever. Pretty soon, the farce would be over, and he needed to get Wil out of the cold, but Rhys wanted the moment to stretch on. "I'd tell you to step on my feet to protect yours, but you'd probably crush them."

Wil hummed. "My father used to let me step on his toes. We'd waltz around the ballroom to Mozart for hours on end."

"Sounds nice." He could see Wil as a gangly young boy, twirling to classical music, candlelight turning his dark blonde hair to gold. "But you're not a boy anymore, and I'm not your father." God. So far from his father.

"No." A thumb stroked the bare skin above Rhys' neckline. Just once...and then it was gone. "I'd never confuse you for that."

"Thank goodness." Something they could one-hundred percent agree on.

Chapter 12

Wil

Wil should move out of Rhys' arms. He knew he should. Any minute, Rhys would realise he wasn't treating Wil like his butler, and he'd withdraw.

It must have been hyperthermia, Wil thought. Not just threatening his fingers and toes, but his brain function as well. Making him do stupid things, like turn in Rhys' arms and press his back to Rhys' chest. The warmth threaded through him, directly to Wil's soul.

From their vantage behind the dry-stone wall, Wil could see everything. Police still swarmed. The flashy blue lights still lit the scene like hyperactive gerbils. But a new calm had settled over Buck House.

Did that mean the danger had passed?

Stand down, Rhys had said. It was as though the universe had listened. As though none of it had been real—a scene played out on a movie set—and Rhys, the director, had called "cut".

At a signal from one of the other police officers, Constable Frazer excused herself and made her way across the sodden grass to the kitchen door. She leaned her head in to listen, then reared back and gave a crack of a laugh. When she turned back to face Wil and Rhys, she was grinning like a loon.

"What's the verdict, Constable?" Rhys called out. His words thunder in Wil's ear.

At her thumbs up, Wil felt the breath leave Rhys' body. The balloon of tension pop. Anticipating the loss, Wil's shivers started up again even before Rhys stepped back. What he didn't expect, though, was Rhys' attention to his arse. A swipe at the back of his thigh sent a flock of swallows swirling in Wil's gut. He flashed a questioning glance over his shoulder. "What are you doing?"

"I made you all muddy." Rhys explained.

The swallows dipped away. "That's the least of my worries, don't you think?"

"We're safe. That's all that matters." Rhys shoved his hands into his pockets. "What else are you worried about?"

"Ah, let's see. Number one," Wil raised a finger. "Frost-bite. I enjoy having ten fingers and ten toes. Thank you very much." He raised another. "Number two, I let a bomb into Buck House."

"It was a bogus bomb. Doesn't count."

"Everything counts." Wil raised another finger. "Number three—"

Rhys made a grab for his fingers. "Stop punishing yourself. You were just doing your job."

Just doing my job? "That puts me in my place."

"I don't mean it that way. Besides, if I was to blame anyone, it'd be Miriam." He hooked a pointer finger through Wil's belt loop. "Maybe I should add 'security guard' to your job description. Give you a raise."

"Please don't." No butler who let a suspected bomb through the door was worth his weight in salt, let alone deserving of a raise. "What if the kids had been here, Rhys? I just can't get that out of my head."

"Yeah. That thought is going to stick to me like Velcro. But they're my responsibility, not yours."

"That's not how this job works. I told you that the other night."

"Look. You can't spend your life afraid of the what-ifs. None of us are hurt. The house didn't blow up. And the world is still spinning in the right direction. The only problem I see is that it's ridiculously cold and we're standing out here squabbling about who's responsible when we could be warm inside with answers to all of our questions."

He felt the tug to his waist again. "Fair point," Wil grudgingly replied.

Two of the armoured officers came out of the house, helmets off, followed by Constable Frazer, who hastened their way.

"Are we good to go?" Rhys asked.

"Yes," she said. "A false alarm, by the looks of it. Thank you for your cooperation."

"Thank you." Wil shook the officer's hand, then made directly for the house.

With the kitchen door hanging open for such a long time, most of the cosy heat had escaped, but the Aga was still warm. Thank goodness. He tweaked open the flue to increase the heat.

If he could, he'd have hugged the damn thing, but Rhys had other priorities.

"Come on. Let's check out what Miriam sent. We could both do with some light relief."

The office was a singular sight. The innards of the crate were laid out in a sea of brown paper. And in the centre of it all was a... "What in the world?"

"I thought it might be something like this." Rhys rubbed his chin, grin unchecked.

"Seriously?" Wil squatted down to inspect it closer. "I know you have an incredible imagination, Rhys, but how could you guess your sister would send you a life-size crocodile with a giant alarm clock lodged between its teeth?"

Rhys laughed. "I didn't have to imagine anything. This is straight out of Peter Pan."

"Well, yes, but...a crocodile?" Like a kid in a museum, Wil found it impossible not to touch, and he ran his fingers along the ridges behind its eyes. To think that millions of such creatures lived in the wild. It was so ancient, so instinctual, so governed by animalistic need. Just the thought made Wil's breath hitch. He couldn't look at Rhys. "It's extraordinarily lifelike."

"Syd's going to love it."

Wil whipped around at that. "You're not going to keep it, are you?"

"Why wouldn't we?" Rhys seemed honestly perplexed.

"Uh, because it's a creepy crocodile." He shuddered.

Rhys squatted down beside him and patted the beast between its cold, reptilian eyes. "Sorry croc. Guess you're not for everyone," he said, then traced the bumps and lumps the length of its wide-open snout. "Want to try one of my famous Irish coffees?" he asked.

For a second, Wil thought Rhys was asking the croc for its drink order, then he caught on. Talk about conversational whiplash. "Famous?"

"Only culturally deficient people raised in the backwoods with crocodiles haven't heard of it."

Wil tsked. "I think you need to revise your geography, Mr Buckley. Crocodiles live in rivers or oceans. Alligators live in brackish swamps. Neither live in the backwoods of whatever imaginary place you're picturing."

"Sassy. I like it. Come on."

At the end of the day, Rhys was his boss. So, Wil held his tongue as he followed the man back to the kitchen and watched as Rhys brewed two espressos, poured a generous portion of Irish whiskey into each, spooned a generous dollop of double cream on top, then finished each mug with a shaving of dark chocolate.

He handed one to Wil. "Special delivery."

"God. Please don't even joke about deliveries." Wil took a sip. Then a second. The double punch of coffee and whisky attacked first his palate, then his bloodstream, and his mug was half empty before he paused to appreciate the rich, creamy taste. "My God. Now I know why you're famous."

"Nothing to do with those miserable films I make?"

"I never said miserable."

"You're right. I believe the term you used was dour. There's an adjective to get excited about."

"If all you wanted was someone to stroke your ego, you shouldn't have hired me." Wil's words might have been full of snark, but they came out like oozy molasses. The warmth and whiskey had done their job, chasing the adrenaline and cortisol from his system, leaving Wil boneless, his muscles heavy, and his brain thick as fudge.

Rhys snickered. "I have more than enough people ready to stroke my ego, thanks very much. What I'm missing is someone who'll be so disapproving of everything I've ever made that they'll invite the armed forces to disrupt my entire life. Oh, wait. I've already got one of those. Never mind."

"Drama, much." Wil rolled his eyes, playing into Rhys' joke.

"See? Disapproval at every turn."

"Mm-hmm. It's a burden."

Rhys' quiet huff of a laugh was stupidly thrilling.

Another sip, the liquid heat squirrelling to his core. Wil could feel Rhys' eyes on him as he licked his lips. It was tempting to play it up, but at least one of them had to maintain a professional demeanour. Even if it was a façade. Wil forced himself three feet back and lodged his hip against the Aga. As a source of heat, it was inferior to Rhys' arms, but he didn't have much option, not if he wanted to respect himself in the morning. "It should be *you* disapproving of *me*. Not the other way around."

"Nah," Rhys disagreed. "Not everything can be subjected to forensic testing before it's opened. The only viable way is to be watchful and to respond the best way we know how. Just as you did today. It didn't feel right, and you made an intuitive leap."

"A wrong one." So very wrong.

"Maybe, but it was all to protect me and mine. I applaud that. Besides, you didn't even sign for the package. That was Angel. And I don't blame her, either."

"You'd be willing to risk your own life—Lex and Syd's life—on guesswork?"

"I have to. There's no other choice. And that's why I don't blame you for calling in the bomb squad. Even if it was for a crack-pot crocodile clock."

"Bzzt, alliteration alert."

A flash of amusement crossed Rhys' face before he tossed back the last of his Irish coffee. "On the bright side—"

"There's a bright side?" Not from Wil's standpoint.

"By hook or by crook, this folly will find its way into one of my films."

Wil groaned. "Ban puns *and* bad alliteration? Two wrongs don't make a right, Mr Buckley."

Rhys clutched his chest. "Death by scorn."

"More like death by drama." Wil swigged the last of his own drink and lamented the bottom of his mug. *Will Rhys be disgusted if I stick my finger in and swipe the last of the cream?*

"You want another?"

Yes. "No, thank you." Much more and he'd lose all rational sense.

"Alrighty, then." Rhys tipped his chin in the direction of the hall. "Come on, let's go find the perfect place to put the croc clock."

"You're not actually going to display that thing, are you?"

"Absolutely."

How is this my life? "Staring at that all day is not what I signed up for."

Rhys laughed. "That'd put you in a minority of one. This kind of crazy is what most of my employees sign up for."

Wil shrugged. "Guess I'm special."

"Mm-hmm. Guess so."

Chapter 13

Wil

Two hours later, after Rhys decided there was no time like the present to display the crocodile, he lassoed a rope around the thing's neck, and another around its tail, and strung it up between hooks on adjacent walls in the less-formal drawing room. "I knew those hammock hooks would come in handy one day."

"Where did you learn to lasso?" Wil gave each rope a good yank to make sure the croc hammock was safe.

"Canada. Cowboying is big in Alberta, where I did some filming for *Hell Bent on Heaven*."

Wil narrowed his eyes. "I don't think cowboying is a legitimate word."

"Did you understand what I meant?"

"Yes."

"Then it's legit."

"Oh, really? Shall I write a letter to the *Oxford English Dictionary* and tell them you said so?"

"Excellent plan." Rhys swung one leg over and sat across the croc's ridged back like a horse. He flicked Wil a cheeky grin when the beastly thing held.

"Hmph. Don't you ever obey the rules?"

"Live a little, Wil." Rhys, curse him, winked.

Someway, somehow, he had to gain back some level of control. "Would you please let me change all the clocks in the house to digital?" Wil asked.

"Never. The ticking sound warms the cockles of my heart."

"Your cockles? Seriously? I thought only eighteenth-century Cornish seafarers used language like that."

"Know many eighteenth-century Cornish seafarers, do you?"

"A few, yeah."

"Really? Care to share the specs of your time machine?"

"There was a local historical society near where I grew up that liked to do re-enactments."

Rhys gazed off into the ether as though he was imagining something...something good.

Should I ask? "What are you thinking about?"

"You, as a dashing pirate rogue." Rhys' answer was so immediate, it had to be true.

"That is...never going to happen." Wil wasn't the sort to go rogue. Or be dashing. He was an ordinary, garden-variety, twenty-something butler. Nothing piratical about him. Time to divert the conversation. "I've been considering themes for the Autumn dinner party."

"Great. What did you come up with?"

"My favourite idea so far is 'Celestial'?"

"Hmm...I don't know too many spiritual types." Rhys tilted his head one way. "Unless we're talking Trekkies." He tilted his head the other way. "If we're talking Earth religions, the one person who comes to mind is Harriet, the local vicar. I've only met her once, but she seemed pretty cool. I'd invite her to dinner."

"Oh, ah, I was thinking more of the universal celestial. As in, out there." Wil waved an arm at the ceiling. "In space. They could come dressed like one of your characters in *Hell Bent on Heaven*, or...or..."

"Some other totally made-up alien thing. A creative free-for-all."

"Exactly."

"In space. Love it."

"Okay. Good. Excellent." Success!

"There's a guy I know living up near Marlow who was a backup astronaut for last year's mission to the MIR space station. Jack Reid. Have you heard of him?"

"Are you serious? I was going to ask you if you knew any space-science types. An actual astronaut would be perfect."

"True."

"Is he handsome?"

Rhys stilled. "What does it matter if he's handsome? He's an astronaut. That should be impressive enough."

"Being a bona fide astronaut is more than impressive. I'm just trying to get an image of him. Astronauts have to be both incredibly smart and physically capable. So, he could be a nerdy geek, or a hunky geek."

Rhys eyed Wil. "I'd call you out for stereotyping, but..."

"But you won't, because it's true."

"I suppose you prefer a hunky geek."

"Now who's stereotyping? And stop fishing for...whatever you're fishing for. I'm trying to get a handle on the guest list. My personal preferences have no bearing on that." If he said it loud enough, it might just be true.

Rhys climbed off the croc's back, then gave its head a pat in thanks.

It wasn't sweet.

At all.

Wil cleared his throat. "So, how do you know this astronaut guy?" *Nope. No fishing going on here.*

"Like the cowboys in Alberta, Jack consulted on *Hell Bent on Heaven*. He helped me out with some practicalities of space travel."

"Can you give me his details and I'll call him to see if he's free that evening? If he can't make it that night, we could use that theme next year." *If* Wil was still Rhys' butler in the new year. After the day he'd had, the chance of that felt like it was evaporating into the ether.

"I'd better call him first." Rhys said. "I don't know how he'd feel about cold calls from a stranger. After today, you'd have a better sense of how quickly a security breach can escalate."

"True." He understood the man's caution, but it stung that Rhys didn't trust him enough to undertake such a minor task as to make a phone call. "You'll let me know his answer?"

"Will do."

Rhys nodded.

Wil nodded.

And the croc clock ticked on.

"Righty-o, then…" Rhys said, at the same time Wil said, "I'm just going to…"

Wil waved a hand toward the office, fully intending to leave. Too much togetherness was playing havoc with his sanity. But a butler didn't leave his boss. Not with a conversation unfinished. He clasped his hands behind his back.

Rhys mirrored his posture.

Was Rhys reluctant to walk away?

Why?

"I'll message you if I get an answer from Jack," Rhys said.

Wil nodded his thanks. "I appreciate it."

Rhys shuffled his feet, then stuck his hands deep into his camo pockets. Uncharacteristically hesitant. "I know today was crazy, Wil. But I want to say thanks. For everything." He quirked his lips. "Seems you'll fit in at Buck House, after all."

And there it was—Rhys' hard-won approval.

Wil tried to say something.

Anything.

How sad was it that one tiny compliment could insert a crocodile-sized frog in his throat? Because as much as he craved Rhys' praise, it wasn't enough anymore. As Rhys' butler, his place was on the sidelines. Never belonging at the heart of things. Especially not in Rhys' heart.

Or in his bed.

Shit, Wil. You're such a fool.

Swallowing thickly, Wil gave as dignified a nod as he could manage, then made a beeline for his office. He didn't turn on the light, just sat in the dark with the cold moonlight turning every sterile surface ghost grey.

Moments later, he heard the kitchen door close and, once again, Wil was entirely alone—his world so quiet he could practically hear the grumbles of his forefathers turning over in their graves. Because a butler who fell for his boss was destined for disappointment...or worse.

Chapter 14

Wil

True to his word, Rhys promptly forwarded Jack Reid's acceptance with a plus three. In return, Wil delivered the ugly plaster figurines up the treehouse dumbwaiter with an impersonal 'for your attention' notice. By the time he'd tidied the office and followed Evangeline's elaborate instructions on how to reheat soup, the croc-clock debacle felt like a hazy nightmare.

Would he do anything different if he could?

Maybe.

But Wil's world wasn't like the movies. He couldn't turn back time. There was no green screen to fudge reality, and no editing booth to cut out mistakes. It was pointless to wish for a do-over.

As Evangeline's soup reheated on the Aga stove, Wil looked out the small window of the cavernous kitchen into the infinite darkness of night and replayed the memory of Rhys' arms wrapped around him; his solid chest at Wil's back; his breath skimming the fine hairs at Wil's nape. The contentment Wil had felt at being welcomed to Buck House was huge, but it was nothing compared to the overwhelming rightness he'd felt in Rhys' arms.

No. He didn't regret anything. Except perhaps to remember to put on a coat, scarf and shoes before racing outside into the cold and the wet.

Evangeline's hearty soup warmed his bones and set the final nail in the coffin of his day's energy stores. Wearily, he cleaned up, climbed the stairs to his rooms, and changed into fleecy pyjama pants and a long-sleeve t-shirt.

To combat the late-afternoon gloom, Wil chose an upbeat playlist, then hauled out his well-loved art case for resources to help brainstorm both beautiful and amusing invitation designs for the Celestial-themed dinner party. Maybe, Wil thought, he could print coloured metallic ink on black paper and create beautifully shiny images of distant planets and nebulas, of bright solar flares and streaking comets. A colourful metallic image on black paper with silver calligraphy would be perfect.

That sorted, Wil ticked 'design invitations' off his to-do list with great satisfaction. A job well done always helped him feel centred.

A good start.

Next on the list was to brainstorm decoration ideas.

A starlight installation from the local artist, Lenny Bane, would fit perfectly in the drawing room. He imagined the milky way gently rotating around the walls and ceiling. Then, in the entry hall, he could hang the planets of the solar system—from far-distant Pluto at the front door, to the sun shining bright above the dining table.

Wil added, "find giant gold disco ball" to his to-do list.

Wil thought he'd change up the table decorations and pair tarot card place cards with old navigation instruments. Oxfordshire might be landlocked, but the Thames had brought trade upriver for centuries, so he added "nautical paraphernalia" to the list.

Onto the guest list.

Jack the astronaut and Harriet the vicar were a great start. He liked that Rhys focused on locals, so Wil plugged a few relevant search terms into a local online directory and the guest list that popped out was surprisingly varied. Keeping in the celestial theme, he quickly jotted down details on an astronomer, an astrophysicist, and an astro-geologist, all from Oxford, then added a local astrologer. If they all brought a plus-one, and Rhys brought a date, they'd be half-way to filling the dining room table.

Since food wasn't Wil's forte, and Jacob mentioned they always hired the same chef, he added "celestial menu" and "speak to Evangeline and the chef", too. With any luck, they'd come up with an inspired menu.

After hours of planning and sketching and planning some more, Wil looked at his watch and groaned. The boss mightn't rise before noon, but the butler wasn't so lucky.

"Time for bed, Wil."

He set aside his trusty notebook, switched off the music that had been playing on repeat for goodness how many hours, stretched out of his pretzel position, and crossed the sitting room to pull aside the curtain on his Juliette window. The lamp light behind Wil threw his shadow onto the window and, inside the darkness of his silhouette, he saw a single light gleaming in Rhys' treehouse.

Was he inadvertently mirroring Rhys' body clock? Had living in close proximity made them fall into sync?

Wil grazed his fingers along the side of the glass pane, thinking about how quickly they'd connected. Not as boss and butler, but as individuals. As men.

The light across the way warped as Wil yawned. Well, perhaps they weren't totally in sync.

At their very core, he and Rhys were opposites. Rhys Buckley was his own man, with a drive to bring something new to the world. He wasn't following in anybody else's footsteps. His job wasn't to uphold the old ways. It was to create something new. He wasn't interested in the tried and true. Not like Wil, who'd carved his entire world out of tradition.

Never the twain shall meet.

The reminder was stark. He couldn't have Rhys *and* keep his job. So, it was moot to even contemplate the what-ifs. Why wish for what he could never have?

Wil shook himself, turned away from the glass, and firmed his resolve. He had a job to do, and nothing was going to stand in his way.

Chapter 15

Wil

The following week passed with so little drama that Wil thought the bogus bomb incident might have been a watershed moment in his fledgling butler career. If his parents could see him at work, running Buck House like a slick machine, they'd be proud as hell. Added to that, he barely saw Jacob, which Wil took as a vote of confidence. It was as though he'd had a year's worth of drama in one day and the universe was repaying him with ease and serenity.

He'd familiarised himself with the workings of Buck House as both a home and a business—consulting with Rhys' security company to enhance the procedure of receiving couriered items, and interviewing Jacob's short-list of temporary housekeepers to find domestic help for while Evangeline was on maternity leave.

The young and energetic Georgina Harris would fit the bill perfectly. She was already working part-time in nearby Cantnoor Cross, and was happy to help in the lead up to Evangeline's baby's birth. Evangeline would never admit it, but Wil could tell it was a relief to know she wouldn't need to haul the vacuum cleaner up and down the stairs for much longer.

Whether it was because of Rhys' sleeping habits, or his need for seclusion to get into his *creative flow*, Wil barely saw his boss during the day. It wasn't till the evenings that Rhys came out of seclusion and cajoled Wil into going the extra mile for his job.

"If you're going to work for me," Rhys said midway through Wil's second week at Buck House, "you need educating."

Rhys' arena of education turned out to be cinematic.

"It's a travesty that you only know a handful of movies," Rhys declared at Wil's first lesson. "I'm going to show you my favourites. First up is *The Goonies*. You're going to love it."

And love it, he had.

What better way to spend a couple hours than with a bowl of hot buttery popcorn, a movie that made him laugh out loud while regressing to the age of twelve, and a gorgeous man who laughed with him—still entertained by a movie he confessed he'd seen dozens of times.

Each night, Rhys dragged him into the media room for another dose of 'education'.

Not every film was joyful.

He shed tears over Spielberg's *E.T.*, sat riveted the whole way through Alfred Hitchcock's electrifying *North by Northwest*, and had to prop his eyelids open for Stanley Kubrick's less-than-electrifying *2001: A Space Odyssey*.

For Ang Lee's spectacular *Crouching Tiger Hidden Dragon*, Rhys insisted they replace the popcorn with ice-cream drizzled in heady lowland scotch. The next night, Rhys replaced the sweet treat with two fingers of Islay scotch, neat. "You'll need it," Rhys had insisted. To round out the drama-fest, Rhys chose James Ivory's deeply sad *Remains of the Day*, which should have come with a content warning. Wil got him back by pointing out that the film had obviously influenced Rhys' earlier work. AKA, his dour period.

Rhys had narrowed his eyes. "You want sappy? I'll give you sappy."

The man really was bothersome.

Wil didn't complain, though, because *A Room with a View* was a joy from start to finish.

On their last night before Lex and Syd were due to return home for the weekend of Evangeline's baby shower, Rhys cued up Tim Burton's *Edward Scissorhands*. Two hours later, as the final credits rolled, Rhys touched a finger to Wil's cheek, lifted a shining tear, and touched it to his tongue.

"Why'd you do that?" Wil asked.

"Just checking to see if they're crocodile tears or genuine. Sugary or salty."

Wil dragged his eyes up from Rhys' lips to his hooded gaze. "Do you really think I'd fake such a flood?"

"Nah." Rhys pressed a few buttons on the universal controller, and the room lights rose to a dim glow. "Jacob says my suspiciousness is a natural offshoot of my inquisitiveness. But don't worry, I was just teasing you. Tears like that can only be faked in Hollywood. What did you think?"

"Well, it was weird, but weird in a good way. Like I fell into a giant mixed up pit of charcoal and I couldn't get out."

Rhys laughed. "The first time I saw *Edward Scissorhands,* I looked just as you do right now."

"You mean a pitiful mess?"

"Close to. I remember it exactly. I would have been fifteen, maybe sixteen, when the Oxford Odeon put on a Tim Burton omnibus revival. All his early films. I skipped class to go. Sat in the very un-cool middle row, with a bucket of sweet popcorn and a giant Fanta."

"Sweet tooth."

Rhys didn't deny it. "I was riveted. Barely moved the entire time. I shed enough tears to make that tub of sweet popcorn salty as the sea. Crazy, hey?"

"Sounds life-changing."

"Yeah. It wasn't just the story that had me transfixed; it was the artistry. After that, I was one-hundred percent determined to make films just like it. Quirky and fun; emotionally deep and visually stunning."

"Yeah? What happened between then and now?"

"Oh!" Rhys clutched the right side of his chest. "Burn!"

"Idiot. Your heart is on the other side of your chest." Wil punched his arm.

Quick smart, Rhys grabbed for his wrist, and held on.

Wil stilled and the disquiet of the film melted away.

Was Rhys as aware of Wil as Wil was of Rhys?

Bosses and butlers weren't usually so touchy feely. The boss' physical person was the valet's concern, not the butlers. Perhaps it was just another piece of evidence that Rhys had zero experience working with a butler. Rhys didn't understand the rules—didn't know where to draw the line between professional and personal.

Wil didn't know what to do about it. Or even if he should do anything about it. Not without tipping them over some cautionary ledge. Or without losing his job. Because one thing was certain—he could be Rhys' butler, or his lover. Never both. And something in Rhys' personal touch made Wil think Rhys wasn't aware of a line at all.

Wil tamped down his thrumming desire and edged his arm subtly away.

Rhys didn't seem to notice. "Did you just call me an idiot?" he asked.

Silently, Wil lifted a taunting brow, covering his feelings as best as he could.

"Just for that, next week I'll make you watch David Lynch's entire filmography...starting with *Eraserhead*."

"Should I be scared?"

Rhys leaned in till their noses nearly touched, and he grinned his charmingly evil grin. "Petrified."

Fuck. I'm doomed.

Chapter 16

Rhys

The golden glow from Wil's Juliette window streamed across to Rhys' treehouse, casting gold angel light on the stubborn leaves that still clung to the oak's branches.

It surprised him. Wil wasn't usually up so late. Rarely past the witching hour, and never still at...Rhys glanced at the cuckoo clock on his rough wooden wall...nearly two o'clock in the morning.

"What are you up to, Wil?"

A trial period was one thing, but Rhys hadn't intended Wil to work himself to the bone. If he didn't rest, he'd crash, and then Rhys would have no PA, no housekeeper, *and* no butler.

Selfish much, Buckley.

His rush of happiness when he discovered that Wil actively disliked his films had come as a total surprise. Sure, his ego felt battered, but the challenge of impressing his far-from-sycophantic butler was too good to pass up. He'd goaded Wil into relaxing every evening over a movie, saying it would help him feel better connected to Buckle Up Productions.

What Rhys hadn't expected was the deeper connection he felt in return. Rhys shared his world of film and Wil shared his unfiltered opinion. Occasionally he looked at Rhys as though he had three heads, but more often than not, Wil got him—he understood Rhys' creative leaps of logic. And even though Rhys had more than enough work to hole up in his treehouse for months on end, he kept prodding Wil into yet another movie.

Rhys tried to stay away from him during the day. He really did. But, when he heard Wil ask Jacob where he could source wire mesh and old newspapers to make papier mâché decorations, Rhys couldn't help weighing in. The ten-year-old in Rhys wanted to put a hand up and say, "Pick me!". Instead, he oh-so-casually suggested that it might be fun for Lex and Syd to get involved while they were home for the weekend. He didn't stop to wonder why he was keen for the three of them to spend time together, but it twisted something in him to see Wil wince at the idea.

Did Wil not like his kids?

That made no sense.

In the short time they'd spent together, Lex and Syd had responded well to Wil. His niece and nephew were superb judges of character, and it was hard for Rhys to imagine that they'd read him so wrong.

No. It had to be something else.

The celestial party was Wil's baby, so perhaps he felt the need to retain a sense of control. Having grappled with creative control throughout his career, Rhys understood the direct link between individual effort and reward, and sympathised with the instinct to hold the reins a little too tightly. Wil needed to relax a bit, so Rhys' suggestion to involve the kids wasn't just for them, it was for Wil too.

Late Saturday morning, he descended the stairs to find Lex and Syd and Wil, taking a side each of the kitchen island, surrounded by a mess of wire and newspaper and glue and sprays of glitter that Rhys knew he'd be finding in nooks and crannies for weeks, months...probably even years. He lurked in the doorway, watching and listening and wondering where his fussy Wil had gone while Lex and Syd tried their best to impress him with their stories and antics. "...and then Tris and Shane had to kiss, because that's the rule when you stand under mistletoe. It was so hilarious." Lex puckered up.

"Eww!" Syd stuck his glittery fingers in his ears.

The adage about protesting too much came to mind. Seemed his nephew had a hidden romantic streak.

"Booooring!" Syd whined.

Yep, a total romantic.

Rhys had to press a hand to his mouth to stop his laughter. He was about to reveal himself when Wil said, "Kissing is so not boring. Just you wait, Syd Buckley. One day someone is going to lay a smacker on you and you're going to love it."

"No, I won't."

"Yes, you will," Lex got in on the debate.

"I will not!"

"Will so!"

"Will—"

"Enough," Wil said calmly, halting Syd mid-protest. "If you rub each other the wrong way too much, you're both going to get glitter burn."

"What's glitter burn?" Came the predictable question, thanks to Lex.

"It's like salt rub you get after being at the beach, but you get it from glitter. Now, Syd, show me how this ring contraption for Saturn is going to work, otherwise our universe is going to look ridiculous."

"I got horrible salt rub when Uncle Rhys took us to Majorca last summer."

"Then you know how awful it is. Best not to argue with each other anymore then, hey?"

His kids were smart, but it would seem they could be just as gullible as the next set.

"You shouldn't call it a universe, Wil. These planets only make up Earth's solar system."

"I guess that's true," Wil said.

"*And* it's not actually part of a universe."

"Don't be an idiot, Syd," objected Lex. "Of course, it's part of the universe."

"I'm not an idiot."

"Are so."

"Are not!"

"Are..."

"Lex," Wil's steady voice spoke volumes.

"Sorry, Wil."

Rhys marvelled at the natural job Wil was doing playing ringmaster. For a non-nanny, non-father, non-uncle, his butler seemed to have an uncanny gift for communicating with children.

Wil put down his own sphere and focused his attention on Syd. "I'm intrigued. Why isn't the solar system part of the universe?"

"Because it's not a universe. It's a multiverse. It's like a bazillion bubbles squished together."

"Wow."

"Yeah, and each one has different rules. Like in some, there's no gravity."

Lex groaned. "Boring."

"It's not boring. It's awesome!"

"I think it's wonderful that you're interested in such fantastic things," Wil told Syd.

"It's not fantastic. It's real."

Syd's protest made Wil pause, and Rhys loved that Wil took such great care in formulating his response. "I didn't mean that I don't think it's real. I just meant that your multiverse idea sounds incredible."

"It's not an idea, it's a fact. I read about it."

"Okay, then. You'll have to help me out here, Syd. What am I allowed to call it if I want to show I'm impressed?"

Syd mused on that before, surprisingly, Lex helped her brother out.

"Cool. You can call it cool," she said.

And Syd nodded his agreement.

"Alrighty, then. Cool, the multiverse is."

Lex nodded. "You know what else would be cool?"

"What?" asked Wil.

"We could hang little clusters of stars in the doorways. And all the guests would have to kiss under them."

"Oh. Umm. Well..."

"Like mistletoe. Only we can call it star-toe."

It was too good an idea to be squashed, so Rhys revealed himself in the doorway. "That sounds like a brilliant idea, gorgeous girl. So long as I get a smooch from you. No raspberries!" He pecked a non-glittery spot on Lex's forehead and winked at Wil. What would Wil do if he got him under the star-toe?

Syd raced around to him. "Uncle Rhys! You're finally awake."

"I never sleep through breakfast, kiddo. You know that." He nodded a good-afternoon to Wil. "I see they found you."

"We found each other, actually. Lex was 'super-keen' and wouldn't be denied the joys of glitter. And Syd needed a distraction. He's been a great help in making the wire spheres."

"Distraction, huh? From what?"

"Uncle Rhys, can I take the croc clock to school for show and tell? It's way better than the dinosaur knuckle Sam brought last week."

"Sam H. or Sam G.?"

"Sam G. Sam H. says he's got a message in a bottle from Zambia, but I don't believe him 'cause I looked it up and Zambia has countries all around it."

"Not a beach in sight, hey?"

"There's a lake. A big one. But that's not the same as the ocean."

"Right. Maybe he got his countries confused."

Syd shrugged. In his world, you got details like that right. "So, can I?"

"It's pretty heavy, Syd. Why don't you just invite the two Sams to visit it here?"

Syd flexed his skinny arms. "I'm strong. I could lift it."

Rhys squatted down to his nephew's height. "If you can carry the croc clock in your arms, you can take it to show-and-tell." He held out his hand to shake, man to man. "Deal?"

Syd's small hand felt all the sweeter for the glitter and glue combo it delivered. "Promise?"

"Promise." There was no way he could lift the beast.

"Cool!" Syd ran off to the family room, no doubt spreading glue and glitter everywhere he went.

By the end of the weekend, they were overrun with sparkly planets and glitter was turning up in many unfortunate places.

Rhys didn't have the heart to say their efforts looked more like school art projects than professional decorations, but he had the benefit of a professional design department and digital effects crew at his disposal. Wil had used his hands and his imagination, and Rhys couldn't help but be charmed by his resourcefulness.

That evening, Syd and Lex voted to re-watch *The Goonies*, and even though Wil was officially off the clock, he'd promised Lex he'd join them, too. Rhys sat back and let the kids draw Wil deeper into their cobbled-together family. It surprised him how relaxed he felt about it. But there was something about Wil that put the Buckleys at ease. It was patently obvious that the man fit in perfectly.

Was he too good to be true?

Maybe.

But Rhys hadn't got where he was in life without taking a chance.

He cued up the movie. "Ready?" he asked, barely waiting for the subtlest of nods from the audience before he pressed play.

Chapter 17

Wil

"What are you doing?" Wil asked Evangeline, who'd buried her top half inside the huge double-door refrigerator.

"Nothing." Eyes anywhere but on Wil, she crossed back to the kitchen sink, yanked on her rubber gloves, and plunged wrist-deep into the sudsy water.

Wil didn't have the heart to mention the blob of cream dotting her upper lip. The woman deserved a sweet treat after all her help to plan Rhys' dinner party.

Calder, Rhys' usual catering chef, had arrived early-afternoon in his tricked-out stainless-steel mobile kitchen. His slick operation instilled in Wil a great deal of confidence, even if he'd set Evangeline in a snit by declaring her bigger than Buckingham Palace, then relegating her to garnish duty.

In the hours since, Evangeline had sorely tested Wil's diplomatic skills, but he wanted the housekeeper to be involved. He wanted the entire household to share a collective sense of accomplishment. Most of all, Wil wanted Rhys to see him for the super-organised butler he knew he could be. An asset to Buck House. To achieve that end, the evening needed to go smooth as clockwork. For that to happen, he needed the host to be ready.

"Have you seen Rhys?" Wil asked.

"Not recently. He was in his camo gear when he came down for breakfast, but that was hours ago. Don't worry, he'll rock up sometime."

Sometime wasn't soon enough. "But I need him." Wil just about stamped his foot. "Here," he clarified at Evangeline's raised brow. If Rhys didn't play his part, the evening would be a disaster. "His guests are due to arrive in..." He checked his watch for the zillionth time, "Twenty-seven minutes."

"Plenty of time. If Rhys promised he'd be here, he will." She dragged a colander out of the suds, then chuckled. "Speak of the sexy devil." She tilted her chin at the steamy kitchen window just as Rhys came barrelling through the door with an enormous grin spread across his mud-spattered face.

"Where have you been? You've got to get ready," Wil burst out. And that time, he couldn't contain the childish stomp.

Rhys looked him up and down, and the grin only grew. "What's up, Peter Pan?"

Wil looked down at himself, dropped his fists from his hips and tried very hard not to wag his finger at his boss. "Stop trying to distract me with crocodile jokes. What do you think you're doing getting all muddy? If you don't get showered and dressed quick smart, there'll be nobody to greet your guests."

"Isn't that what I have you for?"

"No! Well, yes, but no."

"That clarifies things."

Wil huffed. "A butler does not replace a host. He, or she, is an adjunct."

"Seriously?"

Wil's nostrils flared. "Seriously."

"Seems like it's shape up and put on your monkey suit or go sit on the naughty step, Rhys," Evangeline threw in unhelpfully.

"Seems so." His eyes trained on Wil, Rhys shucked his shoes, leaned sideways to peck Evangeline on the cheek, and rubbed her enormous belly like it was a lucky genie bottle. In stocking feet, he crossed the room and came to a stop a bare foot away from Wil's spit-shined shoes.

By God, he smelled good. The crisp scent of the coming winter clung to his skin.

Rhys reached for the muted silver bowtie Wil had worn as a nod to the theme. Wil knew for a fact that his bowtie was tied perfectly. He'd checked it twice in the mirror. But Rhys seemed to have other ideas. He played with it. A tug here...a twist there...

The rub at Wil's neck made him swallow thickly, and he could see Rhys' eyes trace the movement at his throat. Eventually, when Wil thought he might finally asphyxiate from lack of oxygen, Rhys squared the lapels of Wil's classic black suit. "Looking ship-shape, Wil," he said, then the heat of his hands fell away and Rhys strolled out of the kitchen as though he had all the time in the world.

It was maddening.

Composure and confidence, Wil.

"You right there, buckeroo?" Evangeline asked.

"Uh-huh." Wil cleared the gravel from his throat. "Of course."

"Sure." Evangeline wasn't so easily convinced. "I can assign you a job to do if you need to keep busy. Plenty of garnishing to do here." With a sudsy finger she pointed to the centre island, where dozens of delicate black sesame tuiles were lined up beside a host of mozzarella mini-moons, perfectly even sprigs of dill, and jars of the best beluga caviar—all primed for construction into delicious and dramatic starters.

"God no." Meal prep had never been his strong suit. But organising was. Keeping the troops on task was.

If only you could keep yourself on task, Wil.

He nudged one of the caviar jars till it was perfectly aligned with the others. "Looks like you and Calder have everything sorted in here. Save me one, will you?"

"Sure thing. I still don't understand why you won't join the party. You've put so much effort into this affair, Wil, you should get to enjoy it, too."

"That's not really how the job works, but thanks for the vote of confidence." He needed it. Wil scooted back through the hall, and into the music room where he switched on the atmospheric playlist he'd compiled, and Blue-toothed it to the mini-speakers scattered around the ground floor.

He did a final test-run of the light installation in the formal drawing room, taking a second to marvel at the illuminated milky way that arced across the walls and ceiling. It looked re-markably like the skies over Exmoor from the roof of Mistleth-waite Manor—a sight that never failed to soothe and inspire him. The installation brought the drawing room to life, and

Syd's solar system of planets—dangling in order from Neptune in the entry vestibule, to Mercury, just inside the dining room—complemented it perfectly.

Inside the dining room, Wil shifted one of the featured antique brass navigation instruments he'd polished to a high shine a smidgen to the left, swept a speck of fluff from the midnight-blue linen that matched the walls, then pulled out his trusty ruler to do a final measure on the table settings, making sure the places were perfectly aligned. If any knife or fork was off its mark, Wil would probably know it in his bones, but he'd take every ounce of certainty he could get.

Finally, Wil turned off the bright overheads and switched on the dozen strings of fairy lights he'd draped from the picture rail across all four dark walls. The pricks of white light sparked like a thousand distant stars—almost as magical as the night-sky over Exmoor—but they weren't the main event. Above the table hung the sun—a giant gold disco ball that reflected a kaleidoscope of shimmering gilt in every single direction.

"Perfect," Wil whispered.

His *pièce de résistance*.

"This looks incredible!"

"Oh, fu—!" Wil whipped around to find Rhys leaning in the doorway. "Don't sneak up on me like that!"

"Sorry," Rhys swept past, barely chagrined. "But seriously. This is amazing. Where on earth did you get this stuff, anyway? Is that a sextant?" Rhys reached across to the table's central tableau and stroked one of the gleaming brass gadgets. "What's this?"

"An astrolabe."

"No idea what that is, but it's gorgeous. What are all these whirls carved in the brass face?"

"It's the constellations as known during the Renaissance period."

"Like the saucepan?"

"More like Pisces and Andromeda." Wil eyed Rhys suspiciously. "Have you been into the booze already?"

Rhys quirked a brow. "And if I had?"

"Nothing." Wil huffed. Rhys was right. It was his house. His party. His bar. He was Wil's boss. The man could do as he liked. Plain and simple.

Rhys leaned in so close Wil could see the silver flecks in his fall-into-them eyes. "Relax, Wil. It was a joke. You might want to prepare yourself for some fun, though. Or isn't that in your butling handbook?"

No more than strangling the boss is.

"I see those fierce claws. Put them away." Rhys grasped Wil's hand and held it like he was Prince Charming preparing to lay a kiss on his Cinderfella's hand. "But seriously, Wil. It's like a space pirate's mecca in here. You've done wonders."

"Don't sound so surprised, Rhys."

"Don't sound so defensive, Wil," Rhys returned. "I know this is a big deal for you, but you need to relax or you'll scare away our guests."

"*Your* guests." Wil rolled his neck, but it did little to relieve his tension.

Composure and confidence, Wil.

The self-talk didn't help at all. Which shouldn't have sur-prised him. With his boss around, both were in very short sup-ply.

Rhys stepped up close behind him and kneaded Wil's stiff neck and shoulders.

"You're not helping," Wil grumbled. If anything, Rhys' touch exacerbated the visceral war between his body and his mind. The want.

After one last press of Rhys' thumbs into the flats of his shoulder blades, Wil forced himself to step away. "Stop trying to butter me up." He didn't have time for the push-pull of teasing-compliments. "Your guests will arrive any minute."

"Do you need buttering up?"

"No."

"Well then, I mustn't have been."

"That's not even logical." Wil huffed at Rhys, then at himself for even bothering to get huffy. He dragged his attention down from Rhys' gorgeous eyes down to his... "What on earth are you wearing?"

"You like?" Rhys struck a pose in his gold lame shirt and platinum metallic suit. It was a get-up even John Travolta would reject. "I was going for a dapper intergalactic game show host."

"What do game shows have to do with celestial?"

"Isn't it obvious? People look to the heavens for answers, but in my experience, the only people who always have the answers are game show hosts. I figure an intergalactic game show host is bound to have the secrets of the universe at their disposal. And since I'm supposed to be the all-wise host, I figured it was perfect."

"That's…" *Ridiculous.* "Semi clever."

Rhys preened.

"But you know you're going to have to explain yourself all night, right?" Wil had to point out.

Rhys hooked his thumbs through his belt and shrugged. "Or I could choose not to."

"Are we back to the arrogant host routine again?"

"Potato-potahto. I prefer the word enigmatic."

That, he was.

Chapter 18

Rhys

Rhys moved from group to group. Inviting conversation amongst his guests. A few of them knew each other, but most were strangers.

"These little planet shots are genius, Rhys." Lillian, Jack Reid's gorgeous wife, circled the drinks display set on a high table in the middle of the drawing room. With the table draped in black linen, the comet-shaped foam tray, pierced with dozens of black golf tees holding perilously balanced jelly shots, looked like it was zooming through space, dragging colourful celestial bodies in its wake.

"Thanks, but this is all Wil's creation. The kids pitched in, but the ideas are all Wil. He did a bang-up job. Don't you think?"

"Wil?" Lillian asked.

"My butler." Why did it feel wrong to call him that? Was it just because it felt weird to say he had a butler? Or was it because it was Wil?

"It's gorgeous," she agreed. "I don't want to mess it up by taking one."

Selina Barrett, the grabby starlet, had no such compunctions, dashing back two in a row. "Wow, Rhys. These are potent. I might have to bunk in with you tonight." She took another.

"Steady on, Selina." Rhys edged away from her. Selina was an excellent actress with a bright future in the industry, but if she thought the best way to land a role in one of his films was to get up close and personal, she was sorely mistaken. It may have been his idea to invite her to his dinner party, but Rhys did *not* want Wil to see him getting cosy with the woman. He didn't want to get cosy with anyone. No one except Wil.

Rhys chose an iridescent shot and clinked his tiny spherical glass to Lillian's. He spied the genial astro-geologist nearby, "Hey, Sam, do comets separate out into baby comets? Cometlets?"

Sam laughed, his cheeks already well beyond rosy. "I guess they do now." He lifted a golden jelly sphere from the display. "You'll have to introduce us, Rhys. Where is this genius butler?"

"You already met him when you walked in the door tonight." Rhys lifted his comet shot. "Cheers," he said, and the rest of the party followed suit.

Wil's ears must have been ringing because he appeared at the door of the drawing room and announced, "Dinner is served."

Why is his earnestness so sexy?

Rhys cleared his throat. "Shall we go through, then?" He gestured to Lillian, who was chatting with Harriet, the local Vicar, and Jemima, the astrologer. "Ladies first."

Before Wil could follow the last guest through the hall and into the dining room, Rhys latched onto his wrist and pulled him into the dim space under the stairs.

"What is it? What's wrong?"

Rhys pressed his free hand to Wil's mouth. "Nothing. Everything's fine. It's perfect. You're doing marvellously."

"Then why did you yank me aside? I have a job to do and your date is going to wonder about us." Wil pushed at his chest, but Rhys didn't budge. For reasons he couldn't even begin to fathom, he needed to be close.

"Who? I don't have a date."

"Yes, you do. Selina Barrett."

Why would Wil think that? "Selina is not my date. She's a colleague. Maybe. Although, I'm rethinking based on her performance tonight." He pressed Wil further into the dark hidey-hole.

"I don't think she quite sees it that way."

"Who cares how she sees it?"

"I do." Wil shoved back at his chest.

He backed away a millimetre. "I just..." How could he explain what he didn't even understand himself? "I just wish you could join us. You, more than anyone else, deserve to enjoy this evening."

"You sound like Evangeline. And what makes you think I'm not enjoying myself? I've worked hard for this moment."

"This moment exactly?" Rhys stepped closer again, quirking his lips. He slipped his hands up under Wil's suit jacket, ran his fingers along the top edge of Wil's narrow leather belt, warm from his body heat.

"This evening. You know what I mean. Stop being insuffer-able." Wil's hands flattened against Rhys' chest. His actions very much *not* upholding his words.

"I come by it naturally."

"Tell me something I don't know." Wil rolled his eyes. "And stop stressing me out by pulling me into dim, dark places. I've got a job to do, remember?"

"Dim, dark places can be fun." Rhys smoothed his hands further around and up Wil's back, feeling the tension in his muscles beneath the crisp cotton of his shirt. "You're wound up like a slinky. Let me de-slink-ify you." A kiss. That was all he wanted.

Well...maybe not *all* he wanted.

"Again, with the word-invention. This is your night, Rhys. It's what you asked for. Why are you so set on ignoring your guests?"

"It just felt wrong, not having you there."

"I was there. I am here."

"By my side, I mean."

"So, you said. But that's not how butling works, Rhys." Wil wrestled Rhys' arms out from around him, then brought their hands together. "The only thing wrong right now is you. You're supposed to be in there charming your guests, not accosting your butler under the stairs."

"Kill joy." Accosting Wil was way more fun than making small talk.

The eyes rolled again. "Get over it, Mr Buckley."

"Never, Mr Haines. But since you asked so sweetly, I'll go out there and do as you ask."

"Thank you."

"You're welcome."

Wil manhandled him out from under the stairs, proving he could've done it all along, and hustled Rhys out of the shadows. "Go."

"I'm going." Rhys raised his hands in surrender. He felt Wil's gaze burrow into the centre of his back like a red-hot poker all the way into the dining room.

"Everything okay, Rhys?"

Shit. Selina. What had possessed him to add her name to the guest list? Past-Rhys obviously had zombie mush for brains.

"Everything's perfect, Selina. Let's find you your place."

"I'm to your left."

"Really?" Curse you and your erroneous assumptions, Wil Haines. "That's handy. I wonder who Wil placed on my right. There are apparently rules for these things, but I've never really understood formal etiquette. If I had my way, we'd all be in beanbags enjoying a movie-marathon. But then I suppose we wouldn't have this astonishing table to enjoy. Wil did a great job, don't you think?" He held Selina's chair out and helped seat her, then took up his place at the head of the table. He picked up the tarot card set squarely in the middle of his plate—The Fool.

Rhys revealed it to his guests. "Should I take this injustice to heart, do you think?" He mock-complained to the group, getting a gratifying laugh. "Which card did you get, Selina? The Star? I'm jealous. And, Lillian? Ah…The Empress. Of course. Lovely to have you on my right. Here's hoping you can keep both Jack and my foolishness in line. Have you two met Isla and her husband, Lenny?" He pointed to Jack's right-side table partner. "Lenny created the incredible light installation in the drawing room."

Simon, the young server, made his way around the table, helping the remainder of Rhys' guests into their seats. Wil followed behind, pouring sparkling Champagne into fine crystal flutes.

Rhys clinked the side of his glass gently and the group settled.

"Welcome to the inaugural Buck House celestial dinner party. Celestial is a word that opens itself up to interpretation, and you've all done the theme proud. I noticed a surprising trend amongst the STEM types. Seems black is still in. I expect that from the theatrical crowd, but it's a strong look." He paused for effect. "However, after much deliberation, I award the title of the best costume to our local vicar. Harriet, never in my wildest dreams did I think you would come dressed in fluorescent star flannel pyjamas. Well done, you."

Harriet beamed. "You said it yourself, Rhys. These are my 'wildest dreams'."

"Nice pun. I doubt Jack would admit to it, but that's probably the outfit every astronaut dreams they could wear as they climb into their clunky space suits. You have truly made my night." He raised his glass in a toast and the entire table followed suit with a good-natured laugh. "Here's to an evening of brilliant new friendships and dazzling fine dining." He raised his glass again. "Cheers."

"Cheers!"

Chapter 19

Wil

A Celestial Affair

Menu

Cosmos Comets

— 'out of this world' Vodka shots

Black Hole Fishing

— black sesame tuiles, mozzarella moons, Beluga caviar, and dill

sprigs

Wish Upon a Star

— fresh star-fruit palate cleanser

Verdant Venus Rising

— hazelnut-encrusted Veal medallions, moon-pale mash, and

space-debris salad (garden peas with shaved truffle and goat feta

crumble)

A Soft Landing

— rubble of gold-encrusted honeycomb, meringue, biscotti, and

bitter chocolate, over brandy blancmange

C alder and Evangeline were on fire, delivering dish after delicious dish.

Wil wanted to think they were going the extra mile for him. But he knew their loyalty lay with Rhys. He was just the traffic-controller, shuttling between the kitchen and the dining room to announce each dish, pour complementary wines, and avoid Rhys' eye.

He'd had mini-menus printed on each guest's tarot card, so he didn't have to worry too much about mangling his announcement, but Wil got tongue-twisted on the *tuiles* part of the black sesame tuiles, and forgot every single ingredient in the space-debris salad plated with the tender veal medallions.

FYI, Wil, that'd be garden peas, goats' feta, and shaved truffle.

Course after course—each with a complementary wine—the table grew increasingly merry. On his last sweep with a bottle of rich Viognier, Rhys latched onto his left arm, pulled him down so they were face to face, and whisper-shouted, "Who knew science nerds could be such a riot? I feel right at home."

He ought to have separated himself from Rhys. That would have been the professional thing to do. But something about the daggers Selina was throwing his way made Wil want to throw all sense to the wind and yell, *"Mine!"*

But he couldn't. Not while he was still on trial at Buck House. Not publicly.

If only he could say what he really thought...

If only he could do what he truly wanted...

If only...

But, no.

Their reputations would be in tatters.

And there'd be no going back. For him, or for Rhys.

Trying to be stealthy, Wil pressed the sharp of his fingernails into the back of Rhys' hand. Not to hurt. Never that. But Rhys was three sheets to the wind. His cheeks ruddy...his eyes glazed. It'd take talons to cut through that.

"I'm pleased to hear you're enjoying the evening, Mr Buckley," he said, then tucked his hands behind his back, out of harm's way.

Rhys frowned at his formality, but Wil didn't know what else to do. A butler's reputation reflected on their boss, and if he'd learned one thing since arriving at Buck House, it was that Rhys was a well-respected man within his industry and his community. The last thing Wil wanted to do was mess with that.

Lillian, who sat to Rhys' right, patted his arm. "It's okay, Wil. We all know how free Rhys can be with his affections."

"God, yes." Jack guffawed, and wrapped his arm around Lillian's shoulders. "The first time I met Rhys. He and Lillian were snuggled together in a hammock. Thick as thieves, they were. Like teenagers in heat."

"Hey!" Lillian socked her husband in the shoulder. "It wasn't us acting like teenagers. Tell everyone what you did about it. How much of a jealous man-child you were."

Jack played it cool. "I did what any good husband would do when his wife's honour was on the line—I got out my lightsabre and dared him to a duel."

"Honour." Lillian scoffed. "If I recall correctly, Rhys and I were discussing Dickens' film adaptations. That's hardly worthy of death-by-lightsabre."

"You could have been discussing the adaptation of the *Financial Times* for all I cared. The point I'm trying to make is that you and Rhys were snuggling."

"It was a chilly night," Lillian protested. "Rhys was just being my hot, but totally platonic, water bottle."

"Hot man bottle." Rhys' breath was like silk in Wil's ear.

He resisted the urge to cup his hand around it. To contain the feeling. "Behave," he muttered back, trying not to be obvious about it.

Jesus, Wil, you'd make the world's worst ventriloquist.

Thankfully, Jack barged into their conversation. "The point is, our host is indiscriminately touchy-feely."

"Thanks, mate. Just what a man likes to hear." Rhys laughed.

"Don't make him sound like a letch, Jack. He's affectionate." Lillian clarified. "Not touchy-feely."

Rhys' whole body vibrated with mirth. The fact that Wil could feel it meant either he'd leaned into Rhys, or Rhys had leaned into him.

"Stop," Wil muttered. He should have melted into the background. That was his role—to be available when needed, invisible when not. God only knew what Wil was doing when he pressed in firmer. Prolonging the contact.

"Oh-ho. It's like that, is it Rhys?" Jack shared a grin with his wife. "We approve."

Shit.

Wil peeled himself from Rhys' side, stood to his full height, and pasted on a dignified smile just as Simon appeared in the doorway with a tray of glass dessert bowls.

Thank God for that.

He slipped away from Rhys and retreated to the sideboard, where he clonked the bottle of wine down with zero regard for the beautiful wooden surface. The knots and whirls in the polished wood matched the tangle in his mind, but he spread his hands across the growth rings of the old oak, anyway, as though he could draw in its strength and wisdom through the palms of his hands.

Composure and confidence, Wil. Composure and confidence.

With that little pep talk, he swapped the Viognier for a smaller bottle of dessert wine from the large ice bucket, and returned to his rightful place—a foot beside and a foot behind Rhys' shoulder—to address the party. "For dessert this evening, we have a dish chef likes to call A Soft Landing. Brandy blanc-mange, with a rubble of gold-encrusted honeycomb, meringue, biscotti, and bitter chocolate. To complement, we have a sweet botrytis Rhone Riesling. Enjoy."

With that, Wil melted into the background. The perfect butler—visible when needed; invisible when not. Not a chance that anyone could think anything inappropriate was going on between him and his boss.

Ever.

Chapter 20

Wil

Past the midnight hour, the music morphed into bluesy-jazz and the decanter of cognac dropped to a polite low as, pair by pair, the company thinned, disappearing into the cold, dark night like a reverse Noah's Ark.

After days of intense preparation, Wil was exhausted. His feet throbbed. His back ached. And his shoulders drooped, heavy as lead. If he sat down, he feared he'd never get up again, so he roamed the quieter corners of Buck House, ready for whatever Rhys and his dwindling guests might need.

Accompanied by the hum of joyful conversation, Wil flicked through a few books, then confronted his reptilian nemesis. "I'll always have you, won't I," he patted the crocodile on its snout, "Like it or not."

"Might as well like him, then."

He whirled around and gasped at the sight of Rhys leaning in the doorway. Hands in his pockets. Ankles crossed. Watching. "Don't do that!" Wil clutched his chest like some sort of wilting violet in a swoony historical drama.

"Sorry." Rhys' grin told Wil he wasn't sorry at all.

Caught off guard, Wil snapped, "Did you need something?" Just once he wanted to be the one to surprise his boss, rather than the other way around. To gain the upper hand.

"I've called a couple of taxis for the last of our revellers. Thought you might want to know."

"Already? I thought you'd be going strong for hours yet."

"Nah. According to Chelsey, our astronomer, the moon will rise just short of two a.m. I'm sending them packing before the real moonlight blights our celestial fantasy."

It was a rubbish excuse, but Wil wasn't about to call him out on it. The sooner the night came to a close, the better. He had a date with a pillow. "You didn't have to do that. I have a car service on speed dial."

Rhys tilted his head. "I am capable of calling a taxi, you know."

"I know. But, it's my job." *And I'm having a hard enough time remembering that I'm your employee.*

Rhys tilted his head the other way, then he shifted from his lazy lean in the doorway and closed the gap between them.

Wil didn't move.

He couldn't.

Rhys pulled his left hand from his shiny trousers pocket and pressed it to the space between Wil's shoulder blades. It felt like a brand. *Mine.*

"Come on," Rhys said. "One last push, and then we can collapse."

We.

What could Rhys mean?

The possibilities whizzed through Wil's mind as the pressure of Rhys' warm hand guided him back to the hall, where the remaining guests were helping each other into their coats—a courtesy he ought to have been performing, except Rhys' hand held him hostage.

"Thanks for organising a wonderful night, Wil," said Lillian. "If you ever tire of Rhys' idiosyncrasies, let me know. I'd love to have your help with my event management business. You've clearly got the gift."

"I'm pleased you enjoyed the evening." Wil's words were stilted, but he got them out. Thank goodness for autopilot.

"Next time, you two can come to ours. Then I won't have to find a babysitter."

You two? One plus one did equal two, but there was nothing even about him and Rhys. They weren't a pair. "We're not—"

"Deal." Rhys interrupted Wil's protest. He shook Jack's hand and swung open the front door in a not-so-subtle encouragement to sweep them all out of Buck House. "You don't mind dropping Harriet home on the way, do you, Selina? Thanks ever so much."

"Oh, ah...of course." Selina climbed into the last taxi.

Good riddance.

As the last tail light glinted down the pebble drive, they stood together, waving off their guests.

Rhys' guests, Wil reminded himself.

Not theirs.

Nothing was *theirs*.

Not that Rhys seemed to be any better at upholding that distinction than him.

As Wil pushed the door shut, and the deadlock slipped into place, Rhys' hand slid away. Chasing it, Wil followed Rhys back into the formal drawing room, where Lenny's art installation still speckled the walls and ceiling with drifting starlight.

"Let's have a celebratory glass, Wil. What can I pour for you? Cognac? Or would you rather have a glass of wine?"

"Oh, I couldn't." He started to gather the many used coffee cups and cognac balloons.

"Come on, Wil. Live a little. And put those down. Clean up can wait till tomorrow."

"It wouldn't be appropriate for me to drink on the job." Not that he hadn't already broken that rule a dozen times over. All night he'd felt like he was teetering on the brink. That if he wasn't careful, he might just tip over into unchartered territory.

Free fall.

"Don't worry. I won't tell the boss," Rhys joked. When Wil didn't laugh, Rhys's expression cleared. "You're off the clock, Wil. Relax."

Rhys grabbed his hand and spun him in, Fred Astaire style. It would have been a deliciously romantic moment, except Wil's right foot somehow tangled around his left ankle, he over-twisted, and they both almost went down. "Woah!" Rhys grabbed him around his ribs, held them flush together.

Too close.

"Sorry." *Fuck!* He pushed out of Rhys' arms. What must Rhys think of him?

"It's okay. Remind me not to sign us up for *Dancing with the Stars*, though." He chuckled. "So...that drink?"

"Fine. A smidge of cognac." Anything to distract Rhys from how much he'd made an arse of himself. "But I'll get it."

"No, no. Sit." Rhys pointed at the studded leather sofa. "You've done enough for me tonight. It's time for someone to take care of you."

Flummoxed, Wil sat and watched as Rhys prowled around the room to find fresh glasses and pour two generous serves. The lights of Lenny's universe drifted across his pale face and sparked off his ridiculous suit. He looked like a fucking galaxy.

Mesmerising.

If Wil could, he'd have licked every point those lights touched...and all the points between.

He tugged at the ends of his bowtie to loosen the knot and give himself space to breathe.

It didn't help too much when Rhys crossed the room with two cognac balloons and dropped onto the leather beside Wil, their thighs a hair's breadth apart. "A toast," he said. "To you."

"Me?" Wil sounded breathy. His composure was all but gone.

"Why not? You pulled off a fabulous night. If anyone gets to celebrate, it ought to be you."

"I was just doing my job." Wil took a sip and the rich liquid ochre clung to his tongue.

"Well, then...good job." Rhys clunked their glasses again, then relaxed back on the leather couch.

"I've always enjoyed the feeling of insignificance that comes from being amongst the stars," Rhys said.

Wil was so caught up in his daydream that Rhys' voice made him jolt with surprise. His cheeks flamed with embarrassment. Not that Rhys noticed.

"Tiny compared to the scale and consequence of the universe."

"Multiverse," Wil corrected. "If we're to believe Syd."

"Ha! Yes. You're learning fast," Rhys said.

"About?"

"About Syd. About my family." Rhys waved his hand around the room. "About the unique crazy that is Buck House."

That was a hot button Wil didn't want to press.

"You seemed to enjoy yourself tonight," Wil said, pulling on the politest of polite small talk, like armour.

"You sound surprised."

"Sorry, didn't mean to make out like you're socially inept."

"I may crave creative solitude, but I'm well-practiced at greasing the social wheels when I have to."

"Not the only thing you're good at greasing." *Wait.* "Did I say that out loud?"

"You did."

"Well, shit." Wil looked into his glass. "Cheap drunk." He inflected his voice up, turning it into a question. Hoping Rhys would believe the excuse.

"Mm-hm. Sure."

"You don't believe me."

"Nope. Not a bit."

Rhys was close.

So close.

"We make a good team," Rhys said.

"That..." wasn't what Wil expected him to say. He held the balloon to his heated temple, willing the cool glass to calm his spinning thoughts.

"Didn't you feel it tonight?" Rhys leaned sideways, his shoulder pressing into Wil's.

Careful. Rhys may not mean what you hope he means. "Feel it?" he asked. Every time they were within each other's orbit, energy hummed between them. The gravitational pull. But did that mean he should take a chance?

Put his heart on the line?

Risk...everything?

Chapter 21

Rhys

R hys' arm tingled from his shoulder to his elbow, where he pressed into Wil's side. "You've been taking care of me all night," he said.

It was true. Wil hadn't let up in his precise ministrations...his attentive care.

"It's my job," said Wil.

That was also true, but it wasn't the whole truth. Rhys could feel it. Wil had gone well beyond the extra mile. For him.

"It's my turn now." Rhys shifted to sit sideways and took the half-drunk balloon from Wil. He placed it on the coffee table, but didn't let Wil's hand go. "I've been mesmerised by your hands all night."

"It's the gloves. They're designed to garner attention."

"It's not the gloves." Rhys tugged on the tip of the white cotton covering Wil's pointer finger, loosening it a smidgen. "Tight," he said.

Out of the corner of his eye, he saw Wil swallow. "Yeah."

He pulled on the tip of Wil's index finger, then his ring finger, and Rhys felt the smooth fabric give, revealing a thin ribbon of skin across Wil's wrist. More than anything, Rhys wanted to taste it, but he stopped himself, knowing that his patience would be rewarded if he put in the time and attention. "I'm learning from you," he said.

"How's that?"

"Patience." Rhys skimmed his fingertip exactly where he longed to place his tongue, making Wil's breath stutter. "Attention to detail." He tugged on the glove tip of Wil's pinkie, then crossed back to his pointer finger and thumb.

"Those are virtues."

Rhys gave a breathy laugh. "Not much virtue going on in my mind right now."

"Oh?"

"Yes. *Oh*." Rhys returned his attentions to Wil's index finger and tugged until the whole thing gave, revealing the corded tendons and dusky veins that ran the length of Wil's hand.

Sexiest strip tease, ever.

As the material cleared Wil's knuckles, Rhys brought the back of Wil's hand to his lips for a soft, tip of the iceberg, kiss.

Wil gave a breathy laugh. "This must be what it feels like to be the belle of the ball, seduced by a rakish gentleman."

"You're definitely a beauty to my balls, but I, sir, am no gentleman." He kissed Wil's hand again, then dragged the sensitive inside of his lower lip across the velvet-smooth skin, making it shift over the flesh and bone beneath. Like foreskin, only...not.

Done with the tease, Rhys yanked the glove fully off, not caring where it went. What mattered was Wil. The man beneath the pristine gloves. And Rhys wanted him. Badly. He wanted messy. He wanted real.

Already sitting sideways on the sofa, it didn't take much to pull on the twin tails of Wil's loosened bowtie and drag him down, till Rhys' back was flush with the studded leather and Wil's weight pressed into him. Legs tangled. Chest to chest. Conceding whatever upper hand Rhys might've had. Not that Rhys cared. Power plays had never been his jam.

"Better," Rhys said, blissed out as a puff of Wil's breath mixed with his own.

"Warn a guy," Wil grumbled, but there was no mistaking the interest in his pants.

Rhys flexed his arse cheeks and arched up, reinforcing the point, and circled his arms around Wil's waist. "Touch me," he said.

And Wil did. He cupped Rhys' nape with his bare hand and skimmed the bristled edge of Rhys' jaw with his thumb.

It wasn't enough.

"Kiss me," Rhys said. Aching for a taste.

Wil's gaze honed in on his lips. So close. Not close enough.

"Dying here," Rhys whined.

Wil's eyebrow went up. "I thought you were practicing the virtue of patience."

"Screw that." He lifted to bridge the gap, and captured Wil's lips, claiming him.

Finally!

As much as he'd been the one to take the initiative, Wil was with him all the way. While Rhys' lips roved and nipped, Wil's fingers laced through his hair, cupped the back of his head, and locked Rhys in.

"Mmm." Greedy, Rhys licked into Wil's mouth, tasting the sweet nectar on his tongue. He could get drunk on the man if he wasn't careful.

Still, it wasn't enough.

As he slid one hand lower to sneak under Wil's waistband, he planted one foot on the floor and arched up. And even though there were far too many layers between them, he could still feel Wil's rod. The heat. Needing to be closer, he shimmied his other leg out from where it had wedged under Wil, pulled up his knee, and hooked his ankle around the back of Wil's thigh.

"Mmm." It was Wil's turn to moan, and Rhys ate it up.

He ran his splayed fingers down either side of the nobs of Wil's spine, pressing him closer. The room spun with stars, and it was like nothing and everything had changed in his universe.

"Want you," he said. But then Wil's lips left his, travelling down to buss his chin, skim along his jaw in a whisper-light touch, and nip at the soft shell of his earlobe.

"Rhys." Wil breathed his name, and it was music to his hears.

"Fuck me." He squeezed his leg tighter around Wil's thigh, undulating his hips in a dance old as humankind. Two pulsar stars in delirious harmony.

But Wil didn't do the same. He'd stilled.

"Rhys." The fingers tangled in his hair loosened.

Rhys hitched his leg higher, gripping tighter, and they both groaned. But he could feel the new tension in Wil's spine. The growing distance between them.

"Rhys," Wil's hot breath caressed his ear again, but it wasn't like the last time. "What are we doing?"

"Uh…" Was it not clear? It'd been a while since he'd tried to seduce anyone, but he didn't think he was so rusty that his intentions were unclear.

Wil flattened his bare hand beside Rhys' shoulder and gloved hand on his chest, and pushed up. "We have to stop."

"Why?" Rhys let his knee drop to the side and levered himself up onto his elbows. "What's wrong? Are you okay?"

"You're my boss. I'm your butler. This can't happen." Wil rolled off the sofa.

Everything about him was askew—his shirt half pulled from his trousers, his bowtie dangling long, his stylish quiff as mussed as Rhys had ever seen it.

Rhys wanted to muss him more.

The music must have stopped sometime between the first kiss and the last, but Lenny's starlight still shimmered around the room. It brought an eerie glow to Wil's skin as he busied himself, tucking in his shirt, straightening the line of his jacket…not meeting Rhys' eyes.

"What's wrong?" Rhys repeated the question.

"Nothing. Just…"

"Just, what?"

"I don't blame you." Wil busied himself, tucking in his shirt and straightening the line of his jacket, not meeting Rhys' eyes. "But this—you and me—cannot be. You're my boss. It's unprofessional, perhaps even unethical, for us to be intimate."

Unethical? What the hell? "If I ruled out relationships between staff, most of my employees would be lonely singletons."

"But you're not just one of the staff, Rhys. You're the boss; the top dog; the...the..."

"The one with all the power in this relationship," Rhys said flatly.

"Exactly."

For the first time, Rhys realised they hadn't been in the moment together. Where he'd been envisioning a night of tender closeness, Wil had been thinking...what? Rhys didn't know. Loneliness snuck in. "Have you learned nothing tonight, Wil?"

"What do you mean?"

"I mean, I may be your boss, and you may be my butler, but, right here, right now, between you and me," he motioned between Wil and himself, "it's you that has the power."

"Don't be ridiculous."

"It's true." Rhys grimaced as he adjusted his pants while, ever the diplomatic butler, Wil pretended not to notice.

Wil shook his head. "There has to be a line somewhere, and I'm drawing it here."

"What are you trying to say? No hanky-panky?"

"I'm saying that this was wrong. It can't happen again. Our relationship must remain professional." Wil crossed the room and swung open the door, letting in a shard of golden light that ripped through the stars. "Goodnight Rhys," he said, and closed the door on the way out, plunging Rhys into starry darkness.

"What the fuck?" Stunned by Wil's rapid-fire turnaround, Rhys flopped back onto the couch and covered his eyes with his arm. "And, cut."

Chapter 22

Rhys

H and in hand, he and Wil drifted through the Horse-head nebula to an electronic orchestration worthy of Kubrick, wearing oxygen bubbles over their heads and matching silver hot pants.

It seemed perfectly reasonable that they'd be floating in space together, but some part of Rhys knew it wasn't real. Wil would never wear that get-up.

Dream-Rhys wanted to cling to the blissful feeling, but as his conscious mind took over, the dream segued into very real memories of Wil's quickening body...the shakiness of his breath...the salty taste of his arousal...the deep sense of connection between...

"Fuck."

Never mind wet dreams. Real life provided more than enough fodder to make his morning wood impale the mattress. His bedsheet might have been as white as Wil's gloves, but it didn't hold a candle to real live flesh under staid white cotton. And when he'd peeled them off...*fuck!*

Rhys flipped over onto his back, spread-eagled his legs, and palmed his needy cock.

If only he had x-ray vision—he'd be able to see through the ceiling to Wil's rooms. It was early yet. Hours earlier than Rhys usually woke. Wil was likely still asleep. Mouth lax on his pillow. His skin bare. His oh-so-proper defences down.

Rhys stroked.

Wil wasn't anything like the model-types, male or female, Rhys usually gravitated toward. He wasn't looking for a leg up in the industry. He wasn't impressed by Rhys' success. He didn't even like Rhys' films, for God's sake. If anything, Wil was an antidote to Rhys' ego—the least likely 'breath of fresh air' Rhys could ever imagine. He was genuine and warm and driven, charming in his intensity. And nice. Wil confounded him with his niceness. Rhys found himself wanting to bring a smile to Wil's face. To please him...entertain him...impress him. Which was wacky. Why on earth did he want to impress his butler? It ought to have been the other way around.

It's because you trust him.

Well, that was pure bullshit.

And a boner killer.

And because he rejected you.

"That's not what happened," he said to nobody.

Rhys shucked off the duvet, its downy warmth suddenly too much.

That's just your pride being pricked, Buckley.

Uh-huh. Pricked by a thousand tiny feather quills.

He rolled out of bed and crossed to his balcony. Wisps of early-morning fog shrouded the garden, so still it might've been a photograph. Except movement in his peripheral vision set the mist swirling. A figure. Tall. Posture-perfect. Striding out toward the dry-walled garden.

Only one person walked like that—with cut-crystal purpose and zero swagger.

Wil.

The long tails of his coat flared in such a way that Rhys was sure he hadn't buttoned up. Which meant he'd rushed out. Which meant he was bothered.

Bothered by what?

Could it be Rhys' misfired attempt at seduction?

Would he descend the stairs and find an empty house and an "I quit!" notice signed by Wil?

Had one kiss ruined everything?

It wasn't just one kiss, Buckley.

Rhys closed his left hand in a fist, and the remembered feel of Wil's velvet hardness rushed back, fresh to his keyed-up senses.

But it was not to be.

Which was a good thing. Rhys' life was more than complicated enough already. Despite his initial reservations, employing a butler had proven to be one of his better decisions. Wil fit in at Buck House like a hand inside a glove. "Not your glove...or your hand," he said to Wil's distant back, as though the man might A., hear, and B., care.

"Buck up, Buckley." He turned away from the view, stood under a hot shower till all but the splendid memories washed away, then pulled on a comfortable pair of twice-worn jeans and his favourite hoodie.

Reality had never been his forte, but face it, he would.

⎯⎯⎯⎯⎯*eee*⎯⎯⎯⎯⎯

"**Y**ou look like hell." Typical Jacob, not holding any punches.

Should he tell Jacob what was going on? Wil had ignored him all weekend, tiptoeing around the house, or taking off for parts unknown. In his dreams, they were hot and heavy, but that stopped the minute he shucked his duvet and faced the unforgiving noon light. If the previous two days were anything to go by, he and Wil weren't even functioning as boss and butler, let alone man and...man.

"Didn't sleep well, I guess," he said. "Have you seen Wil?"

Jacob hitched his thumb over his shoulder toward the office. "On a phone call. Evangeline raved about the party, so I guess he passed the test. I thought he'd relax a little, having proven himself, but he's looking more determined than ever."

"Hmm."

"Enthusiastic to the nth degree. Where're you going?" Jacob nudged the overnight suitcase Rhys had wheeled into the kitchen.

"London. Some issues have come up in the production office."

"For meetings, yes, but not to stay. Or did I miss something?"

"No." *Yes.* Jacob had missed a lot of somethings, and Rhys couldn't decide what to do about it. Should he sweep his attraction to Wil under the proverbial carpet? Or should he lay it all out and risk being judged as a slimeball boss who couldn't keep his dick in his pants?

That's not how it was, Buckley.

He knew that, but he also knew that perception was everything.

His professional reputation might be writ large by the media, but Rhys' day-to-day world usually went un-noticed. If he messed up with Wil, and it went viral, his reputation could fracture irreparably.

Telling Jacob was akin to running the first gauntlet. The man knew him better than just about anyone. Rhys trusted him. He was his go-to man. If there was a solution to the Wil problem, Jacob would probably see it.

Decision made, Rhys grabbed Jacob's arm and pulled him out the back door into what turned out to be a miserable day. It suited his mood perfectly, but Jacob, in a blue oxford shirt, light woollen slacks, and suede loafers, was far from prepared to be hauled into the spitting rain.

"Seriously Rhys?" Jacob backed up onto the doorway flagstone.

"Sorry, it's just..."

"Yes?"

"This thing happened."

"Thing?"

"Yeah...umm." His mind went blank.

"Is there a good reason you've dragged me out here where we're both going to catch our deaths?"

"Dramatic much." Rhys complained, but Jacob's expression said he was having none of it. "I don't want Wil to overhear, okay?"

Jacob raised his hands like he was calming a spooked horse. Which was reasonable, Rhys thought. He felt spooked.

"Calm down. What's wrong? Did something happen?"

Bite the bullet, Buckley.

"I kissed Wil." *And got up close and deliciously personal with his cock.*

Jacob's brows wrinkled. "You what?"

"I kissed him."

"You kissed your butler?"

"Yes."

Jacob stared at him for a few beats, his expression impossible to read. "Did he kiss you back?"

"Yes. Well, sort of."

"He either did or he didn't, Rhys."

"He did. We were...you know," he wrapped his arms around his own ribs in a classic clinch. "But then he said he couldn't because it would cross a professional line, and it all went to hell. Now, every time I fall asleep, I imagine him—"

Jacob grabbed his forearm. "Spare me your wet dreams, Rhys."

"Sorry. So now he's in my bed but not really and I really want him in my bed but that won't happen because he's my butler and I don't know what to do because he's done such a great job but he won't be my lover while he's my butler so now I'm kind of screwed only I'm not screwed because he won't..."

"Stop, Rhys! God. You sound like a teenager."

"Yeah. It's scary up here right now." He tapped his forehead. "So, what should I do?"

Jacob looked over his shoulder into the garden, probably looking for inspiration.

"His concerns are valid."

That wasn't what he wanted to hear. "So...?"

"So, you need to respect his decision. Respect his professional boundaries."

"But you're my employee and I have a personal relationship with you. With Angel, too. I'm closer to her than my sister. What's the difference? Why can't I have both with Wil?"

"Jesus, Rhys. You can't compare us to Wil. If you need me to point out that neither of us has shared your bed, you really have lost the plot." Jacob shook his head. "You just want to have your cake and eat it, too."

"Cake?" He didn't follow.

"You're too used to getting what you want. Have you considered what Wil wants?"

An image of Wil—lying half underneath him, bowtie askew—left Rhys in no doubt. Wil wanted him. Maybe as badly as Rhys did.

Their breath huffed opaque between them.

Jacob shuffled on the worn flagstone in the entryway. "Now that I think about it, getting away to London for a few days is probably one of your better ideas. Just make sure you're back by next weekend. Evangeline will kill you if you miss her baby shower. Wil is an excellent butler, and he fits in here. Think seriously before you mess with that."

Jacob's opinion wasn't out of line, but it wasn't what Rhys wanted to hear.

"Whatever you decide, you need to get it sorted soon. In a few weeks, you're off to Morocco to scout locations, and, in case you need reminding, Wil is supposed to be going with you. This could get messy, fast."

"It wouldn't interfere with our work." Was stubbornness a virtue?

"It would," Jacob said.

"Not necessarily." Sex and butling were two very different skill sets.

"I know you haven't had a lot of romantic entanglements that lasted longer than a film shoot, Rhys, but be smart about this. Is a liaison worth the drama? The potential upheaval? Because Wil Haines isn't the sort to accept casual."

Was Wil worth it?

He thought about how easily they'd meshed. How Wil had protected him and his family. How Wil had bonded with Lex and Syd over glitter and glue, so genuinely interested in their lives.

"None of this is an issue if you're willing to commit..." Jacob left that parting thought open—a vacuum for Rhys to fill.

Commit? "Don't be silly."

While Rhys' mind spun, Jacob turned neatly and disappeared into the warmth of the kitchen, leaving Rhys all alone with his uncomfortable thoughts.

What if, instead of his butler, Wil was Rhys' lover? Twenty-four seven. Day and night. Not a clock in sight.

Serious.

That's what that thought was.

Scarily serious.

Jacob was right. A few days away from Buck House could help Rhys clarify his thought. He mightn't be able to get away from his swirling emotions, but he could get away from their source.

Out of sight, out of mind?

One could only hope.

.

Chapter 23

Wil

R hys had walked out of Buck House with barely a nod in Wil's direction.

Clearly, Rhys didn't respect him, personally or professionally. Turned out, all he'd provided was a warm and far-too-ready body. It was stupidly crushing.

Stupidly, because why on earth had he thought Rhys would develop romantic feelings for him? They barely knew each other. His impact on Rhys' life was infinitesimal...a single star in the night sky.

So, nearly a week later, when Rhys barrelled up the drive in his black Range Rover, with Lex and Syd in tow, Wil resolved to be one-hundred percent professional. Like any decent butler, he would be kind and respectful, but he wouldn't get involved. Not like he had.

Not like before.

Syd and Lex bounded out of the car, slamming their doors and talking over each other a mile a minute. Rhys' ears must have been ringing.

Serves him right.

"Good evening," Wil said. Cool. Professional. He led them into the warmth of the kitchen, where one of Evangeline's flaky chicken and mushroom pies rested on the Aga's warm hob.

Rhys trailed in, his arms full of school bags and sports kit. "Something smells good. I'm starving."

"Chicken pie!" hollered Syd, not waiting to remove his coat before he stuck the big serving spoon into the pie dish and scooped out a massive dollop of filling and pastry.

"Save some for the rest of us, kiddo. Evening Wil. How has your week been?"

Peachy. "Fine."

"Excellent. Let's get these rabble-rousers fed and watered and then I promised them a movie."

"Guess what we're going to watch, Wil?" Lex asked.

"I have no idea." Lex was looking at him expectantly...joyfully...and his stoic façade crumbled. "Do I get a clue?"

"There's a princess..."

"And a prince," offered Rhys with a smug smile.

"Does the princess kiss a frog by any chance?" Wil couldn't help sneaking a look at Rhys.

"Eww!"

"Guess that means no. Is it a cartoon, or real?"

"It has human actors."

"Right, so...let me see...there's a prince and a princess who are real people and there are no frogs in sight."

"Yep."

"Hmm. Can I have another clue?"

"It's *The Princess Bride*!" Syd yelled.

"Syd! You weren't supposed to tell him the answer."

Syd didn't look remotely sorry.

"Really?" Wil asked the kids, stunned by the choice. "You're watching my favourite movie?"

"No," Rhys butted in. "*We* are watching your favourite movie. If you'll join us, that is. Right kids?"

"Yep," they chorused.

"Oh." His plan to retreat to quiet safety gone, Wil couldn't think of anything to say.

"Great." Rhys took charge. "Let's all eat dinner while it's hot, then get into movie-mode. Sit up Lex. You haven't eaten yet, have you, Wil? Can I get you a plate?"

Rhys didn't wait for an answer, just dished a hefty portion of pie up, placed it at the chair where Wil had grown accustomed to sitting, and grabbed another plate for himself. How did their roles keep getting reversed so easily? "You should let me..."

"Don't be silly, Wil. I can serve you a meal. Relax. This is your home, too."

If only. But if Rhys could ignore the elephant in the room, Wil could as well. In fact, with Lex and Syd around, Wil really had nothing to fear. He could enjoy the children's company, then take himself off to his high attic rooms. Alone.

During the movie, he occasionally felt Rhys' gaze focused on him, but with Lex and Syd acting as their chaperone, the night went off drama-free, and Wil called out his goodnights with a relieved heart.

His instructors had cautioned him about the fine line between professional engagement and personal attachment while working in a family's home. He'd thought that since he'd grown up in a working household, he'd skim the line with ease. But the reality wasn't quite so easy.

He just had to hang on. With time, living with his boss would surely get easier.

———— *ele* ————

The next morning Wil welcomed the opportunity to drive Lex into Henley, where they picked up enough cupcakes to tempt a dozen pregnant ladies, while Syd and Jacob stayed home to decorate the house with reams of pink and blue paper hearts.

When he and Lex returned, Buck House was transformed.

"Wow!" was all he could think to say.

"Uncle Rhys must have got out the blower."

"The what?"

"The blower. He got it when the BBC4 studio had a garage sale. It's made to shoot confetti, but you can put bigger stuff in it too."

"Such as streamers?" he guessed. Buck House looked like it'd been caught in an enormous pink and blue spider web.

"Yep."

"Come on, Lex. Let's get these cakes in. I want to see what the boys have done inside."

Someone had scattered paper love hearts on the floor from the entry to the less-formal drawing room. There, the path split around the furniture, then merged to climb up the wall to make a giant patchwork heart made of smaller hearts. And underneath the patchwork heart was a gorgeous white crib, crowned by a hanging mobile of stained-glass hearts.

"Oh, my…" Wil couldn't find the words. The house…the room…everything…screamed love. What would it feel like, he wondered, to be the recipient of such devotion?

"Do you like it?" Rhys' voice came out of nowhere.

"Ah! Don't do that!"

Rhys chuckled. "Sorry."

"You're not remotely sorry."

"No. Not really. It's too much fun to catch you unawares."

"For you maybe."

"Yep."

"You sound just like Lex. It's been 'yep' this and 'yep' that all morning."

His smile creased the corners of his eyes. "Do you think she'll like it? The kids helped me find the crib."

Wil sighed. Rhys was impossible. "Of course, she'll love it. It's gorgeous." Careful of the trail of hearts, Wil tiptoed to the crib and tapped one of the glass hearts, setting the mobile in motion. "It looks handmade. Are you sure it's safe around a baby?" Light gleamed in flashes of pink and blue as the hearts spun lazily around.

"It's safe. I soldered and double wired each connection."

Wil turned to him in surprise. "You made this?"

Rhys nodded.

"Wow."

He must have toiled for hours, working with wire and metal and glass till he found the perfect design with the perfect balance. It would have taken a great deal of patience and love.

This was the man Wil had convinced himself was a figment of his imagination; the man he'd connected with; the man who'd lured Wil into his life; the man who had tenderly seduced him. But also, the man who'd disappeared at the first sign of rejection; who didn't have the patience to wait for Wil to be ready; who Wil couldn't trust with his heart.

"It's beautiful." Wil stroked the railing of the crib. "I'm sure she'll love it. Even more so because it came from your hand."

Rhys stole across the room to stand beside him.

He stared down at the empty crib where a baby would soon sleep, ran his finger along the smooth edge.

"Have you ever thought about it?" Rhys asked.

"About what?"

"Fatherhood. Although, I don't suppose it'd be all that easy for a butler to raise children."

Wil blinked. "Why?"

"Because you live where you work."

He'd never even thought about having kids. It made no sense that he suddenly felt bereft.

"I remember when Syd was born. Lex had already lived with me for a year, but I missed her baby years. I saw her occasionally when Miriam passed through between productions. It's not the same, though. Snatches of time don't nearly compare to the twenty-four seven of caring for an infant. I see this crib and I can't help remembering the three-hourly bottle feeds, the endless hours spent changing and burping and rocking and loving that boy. He was such a happy baby."

"Your sister didn't stay?" Wil couldn't help being curious about his family.

"For a little while. Miriam loves her children, and they love her, but she found motherhood daunting. 'Impossibly difficult,' she always said. I think it was just that she couldn't stay still. Still can't. She's the same as our parents—driven by wanderlust."

"Which you didn't get?"

"No. I got the homebody gene from my grandfather. Buck House is a hand-me-down from him."

"They've always been in your care, then? The kids, I mean."

"Almost." Rhys grinned. "Lex came to me when she was four, and I was twenty-three, Syd was born a year later. It was rough at first. I took them everywhere with me. Thank goodness for Jacob and Angel. They kept me sane. These days, boarding school enables me to work solid during term time, and we rummage along the rest of the time. Not that I'd change anything. If Miriam said she wanted to take the kids, I'd fight her all the way. They're as much mine now as they are hers. And she knows it. We're a family." He paused briefly, then went on. "Speaking of family, I wanted to talk to you about that night. This is possibly not the best time, but..."

"Can we talk later? Evangeline is going to arrive any moment and I..."

Rhys grabbed his hand. "I'm sorry, Wil, but if I wait any longer, this awkwardness will just get worse. I said we're a family, and that's exactly how I feel about us. All of us. The kids, Jacob, Angel, me...and you. You're part of the Buck House family now, too."

"Your family isn't the problem, Rhys."

"I know." His mouth twisted. "Even though I see no reason why we can't be...close, while you continue to work for me. I understand you feel differently. Jacob helped me to see that—"

"You talked to Jacob about us? When?" Wil snatched his hand back, horrified.

"Monday."

"He's known since Monday? I can't believe you! Or him! He didn't say a thing to me." Any minute, the world would open up and swallow him whole.

Please, world.

"Jacob's a gentleman. He was even supportive of your choice to not..."

"To not sleep with you while you're paying me? Why thank you Jacob, so glad you approve of my choice to not pimp myself out to my boss." His words were ugly, but Wil didn't regret them.

"Pimp yourself out? That is so not what happened. Yes, you work for me, but we're adults. Surely, we can come to some kind of understanding."

"An understanding?" Had Rhys not learned anything?

"Exactly. If you don't think being together is a professional conflict of interest, then we'll need to make a change."

Wil's heart clenched. "Do you mean...?" Was Rhys going to fire him?

"I've never met anyone who infuriates me more than you do, and that's saying something. You tell me when to take a hike. And I can see you want to tell me to take a hike right now."

Yes. Yes, I do.

"But that's because you don't seem to understand how badly I want you in my bed."

Was the man serious? "You want me, so you're firing me?"

"No! I want you to be with me *and* to work for me. But you won't do that."

"It's my fault that you're firing me?" This was too much.

"No, that's not it at all."

"I can't believe you're firing me because I won't sleep with you. Just how much of an arsehole are you?"

"I never said that. I—"

With astonishingly bad timing, Syd ran into the family room yelling, "Uncle Rhys, Uncle Rhys! Evangeline peed her pants!"

And Lex ran in close after. "She's popped! Uncle Rhys! I'm going to be an aunty!"

"Oh, hell." Rhys groaned. "The baby."

Chapter 24

Wil

T he sight of Evangeline sitting in an oversized flower pot, clutching at her belly, with tears tracking down her cheeks, was the wake-up call Wil needed. Whatever was between him and Rhys was nothing compared to the needs of Evangeline and her baby.

Thinking quick, Wil dashed back inside and grabbed the Range Rover keys from their hook in the entry. "Here!" He threw them at Syd, since Rhys had Evangeline in his arms. "Rhys, take Evangeline and the kids to the hospital. Lex," Wil turned to the girl. "Can you call Nick and Jacob? Tell them what's happening."

Lex nodded. "Is she going to be alright?"

"I'm sure they'll take excellent care of her at the hospital. Here are your coats." Wil piled them into Lex's arms. "How about you and Syd get in the fold-down seats in the back? Your uncle will need your help when you get to the hospital." Wil turned back to Rhys. "Go. I'll lock up the house. Be right be-hind you."

"Wait!" Rhys called out, but Wil was already halfway up the stairs, and Evangeline's scream drowned out anything else Rhys might've said.

Heart racing, Wil scrambled in his attic rooms for his keys and wallet, set the alarm, and locked the house before he jumped in his rust-bucket of a car and headed south. The city of Reading wasn't all that far, but the wet-slick roads were a hazard to anyone who rushed the corners. Fifteen minutes later, he passed through the city centre, eyes peeled for road signs to the hospital.

When the blue 'H' came into view, he stared hard at it, then passed it by. The road blurred, but he kept on driving. When the road intersected with the M4, he could have used the giant roundabout to reverse direction and head back. To the hospital. To Buck House. To Rhys...

But he didn't.

What was there for him? Aside from a family he'd grown to adore?

Broken promises?

Fired. He couldn't believe it. It didn't matter that Rhys hadn't actually said the words. Call him old-fashioned, but he couldn't countenance being both butler and lover, so whether Rhys had said the words "you're fired" or not, the point was moot. If he fell into Rhys' arms again, his career would be dashed before it could even really begin.

What of his self-respect? And what of his heart? No matter how desperately his body might want to say yes, yes, and yes again, his heart needed protecting, too.

Wil tried to blink away the scorn and the anger and the hurt. But it didn't work. How could he have admired the man? Respected him? Trusted him? Liked him? Maybe even...no, not that. His eyes burned as he took the slip road onto the wide motorway stretching west, heading further and further away from Rhys. A blank slate. He took one last look in the rear-view mirror, then pressed the accelerator, heading west into the cold and the grey.

The miles ticked over, hour after hour. The weak autumnal sun dropped over the Bristol Channel and the turnoff to the M5 led him south west through Somerset and into the West Country.

The closer he got to Devon, the more his thoughts took on his mother's scolding voice.

What were you thinking, Wil?

Good question. And what was he doing thinking running home would help?

He'd up and left everything at Buck House—his career, his possessions, his heart.

Jesus Christ. Love at first sight isn't real, Wil.

The memory of Rhys decked out as a Halloween harlot came to mind.

Make that love at second sight.

"Ugh." Wil slapped the steering wheel, but his mind kept whirring. Going over and over every moment of his time with Rhys. Damn the man. If only he could fall into a fugue state and autopilot his way to safety.

Another hour in, Wil pulled his rust bucket into a rest stop to refuel and check his phone.

His notifications were full of "where are you?" text bubbles from everyone under the sun, followed by an isolated "are you okay?" from Jacob, then a picture of a grimacing Evangeline, with fire in her eyes and a death grip around Nick's hand.

I should be there.

But he couldn't be. Not without giving in to Rhys. Not without losing his professional integrity.

He angrily wiped away tears with his coat sleeve, then typed a return message to Rhys. "I appreciate the opportunity to have worked at Buck House. However, due to irreconcilable differences, as per the bounds of our trial contract, I resign forthwith."

Send.

Fuck!

He silenced his phone, climbed back into his pea-green Fiesta, and gunned it west into the wilds of Exmoor.

No need to be polite now—on the road, or anywhere.

Chapter 25

Rhys

R hys read the message on his phone. "What the fuck?"

"Hey. Keep it down." Jacob pulled him into the far corner of Angel's hospital room. "The only person allowed to swear in here is Evangeline."

"He quit, Jacob."

"Who quit?"

"Wil."

"He quit? Why? What did you do?"

"Me?"

"Who else, Mr Lothario?" Jacob grabbed his phone from Rhys' hand. "What did he say?"

"He thinks I fired him."

Jacob frowned. "Why would he think that?"

"It's not my fault. He wouldn't listen, and then we were interrupted, and then…"

Jacob looked up from the phone. "What did you say to him, Rhys?"

"I was trying to be sensitive..."

"Mm-hmm."

"And point out that since he has a moral issue against us getting..." He looked around to see if little ears were in range. Lex was close, so he leaned in closer to Jacob and whispered, "Up close and personal—"

"Please tell me you didn't say that. Look, Rhys, I know you live in the twenty-first century, but Wil's old school. His parents run a vast estate in Devon, and they raised him to respect the upstairs-downstairs divide. I know you're no toffee-nosed lord of the manor, but you're still his boss."

"I know. That's why the best solution is for him to stop being my butler, so we can—"

"Are you serious?" Jacob interrupted again. "You can't make Wil choose between you and his job."

"That's not what I meant. He could still do the job, just not—"

"Get paid for it."

Why did Jacob sound so affronted? "Better that than think he's getting paid to shag the boss. I mean, since that's his issue."

"Don't be a petulant arse. It doesn't suit you."

"Petulant arse?" *Wow, Jacob. Tell me how you really feel.* "Look, the way I see it, umpteen people could be my butler, but there's only one Wil."

Jacob straightened. "Did you tell him that?"

Rhys thought back to their conversation, and the fraught way it ended. "No...not exactly. But he must know. I want more from him than spreadsheets and spit-shined shoes. Different things. And he does too. I know it. Shit. If anything, I offered him a promotion."

"Really? You want to promote him from butler to professional bed-warmer? Correct me if I'm wrong, but I think that job description went out of fashion in the Edwardian Era." Jacob paced across the hospital room, his shoes squeaking on the linoleum floor. "So, where is he now?"

"I don't know. He was right behind us. And how he's...gone. That's why I'm so worried." It was an alien feeling. In all the time Rhys had known Wil, he'd never had to worry about anything. Except maybe during the crocodile incident. They'd bickered, sure, but never seriously. Whether lingering over a coffee, or teasing each other over a movie, time with Wil had always felt effortless—in harmony. Just the thought of how they'd moved together that night had his entire body humming. If he was a musician, maybe he'd understand it better. All he knew was he wanted Wil. The closer, the better.

"How much do you want Wil in your life, Rhys?" Jacob broke into his reverie, unknowingly reiterating his own thoughts.

"I just want him, all of him." Rhys glanced across at his family. All so bright and happy. "He fits. You know? With us."

"Then you need to go fight for him. And you need to be smart about it."

Lex must have felt his attention. "What's going on?"

"Your uncle's realising he's in love."

"What? No. I'm not." That was going way too far. "Nobody falls in love within a month." Ridiculous notion.

"Syd, get over here." Lex waved her brother over from where he'd plastered his face to the hospital window. "Evangeline will want to hear this, too."

Rhys looked around for a hole to hide in. Where was CGI when a guy needed it?

"What's going on?" Asked Nick.

"This is none of your concern." No way was he spilling his heart to Angel's boyfriend. He'd never been part of the Buckley inner circle.

"Uncle Rhys loves Wil." Lex oh-so-helpfully explained to the entire room.

"I didn't say that." Did nobody ever listen?

Lex ignored his protest. "What did he say when you told him? Where is he? I thought he was coming to the hospital? It's been hours."

"He was," Rhys said.

"But now, he's not," Jacob clarified.

Bloody Jacob.

"Why not?" Syd asked.

"Because I—"

"Because your uncle is emotionally stunted. But he's going to fix it. He's going to lower his drawbridge, and let Wil in. Right, Rhys?"

Easy for you to say.

"Psychological warfare isn't fair," he grumbled. It was hard enough to admit to himself that he'd screwed things up. Admitting it to the kids was ten times worse. And to Angel. Fuck. He'd never hear the end of it. Good thing her complete attention was on baby Poppy. Or so he thought...

"What's going on?" she asked.

Ugh.

"Uncle Rhys fell in love with Wil, but he stuffed it up, and now he has to fix it," Lex oh-so-helpfully explained.

"Succinct, but true," Jacob said.

"Finally!" Angel grinned.

Jesus. "Does everyone here get to have an opinion?"

"Yes," they agreed as one.

"Ugh." With family like this...

Ten minutes later, with Angel's blessing, he and the kids were on the road.

First, they went home, but Wil's junk of a car was gone and all but the security lights were dark.

He quickly nixed the idea that Wil might have gone anywhere else local. Since moving to Buck House, Wil claimed he loved Hewstoke Woods and the surrounding Chilterns, but, clearly, it wasn't home to him. Not yet. And, while Wil had studied to be a butler in London, Rhys didn't see him running to the city to nurse his hurt. Wil's stories of home had always been about Devon.

One quick call to Jacob elicited a promise to find the address of the estate where Wil had grown up. In the meantime, he plugged Exmoor into his navigator and followed the crescent moon west.

They lost Syd to sleep pretty quickly, but Lex lasted well into the drive, asking a multitude of questions that all amounted to, "What will you say to get him back?" The only answer that quieted her interrogation was, "I don't know, Lex. Let's hope actions speak louder than words."

Eventually, the darkness and the purr of the road lulled Lex to sleep, leaving Rhys alone with his regrets. Hour after hour, the odometer ticked over, closing the gap between him and Wil. Or so Rhys hoped.

In truth, Rhys didn't know what he was going to say to win Wil over. He was a creative. He usually had no trouble coming up with persuasive ideas. But Wil confounded him. He was different. Special. And Rhys suspected that the only way to convince him to come back was to buck up and tell him the truth.

We fit together, like a hand in a glove.

God. What a sap.

As midnight approached, his phone lit up with a message from Jacob with Wil's parents' address. He pulled over at the nearest rest stop to plug in the directions and followed the app's arrow through miles and miles of undulating, starlit wilderness. Rhys was just starting to wonder if they'd run out of road and accidentally drive into the sea when the Range Rover's headlights lit on a gate house beside a set of impressive sandstone pillars, the left one etched with the place-name, *Mistlethwaite Manor*. The filigreed ironwork gates were open, so Rhys drove across the teeth-chattering cattle grid and up the long gravel drive to a matching honey sandstone pile that was so massive the Range Rover's headlights barely lit a quarter of it, even on high beam.

Rhys' seatbelt tugged across his chest as he leaned forward in an attempt to take in the whole thing in at once. "Jesus Christ." His breath frosted the front window. "No wonder Wil described Buck House as cosy." The place was a fucking castle.

Beautiful cut-stone walls gave the house a deep solidity, as though it were born of the earth and bound to it. Was this what it felt like to be landed gentry? Unlike Miriam, he'd always wanted a place where he belonged. Buck House was his dream come true. But Mistlethwaite Manor was something out of a fantasy.

Twin lamps straddled the buttressed front door, but the golden light shining from three low windows on the far-right of the building looked far more welcoming. Rhys drove as close as the wide turning circle would allow, then pulled on the handbrake and shut off the engine, noticing for the first time the wind that whistled around the car. The West Country was known for its gales off the Atlantic, but he'd been lulled by the solidity of the Range Rover. With the engine off, nothing could stop the chill of night bleeding through, making him shiver.

The witching hour.

Ordinarily, he'd be a fan of the dark. But there was just so much of it. Pressing in on him.

Rhys flicked on the internal light, wishing all of his problems were so easily fixed.

"Hey." He gently shook Lex's shoulder. "We're here."

"Here...?" She rubbed an eye with the heel of her hand.

"Uncle Rhys?" Syd's voice was small. "Are we there yet?"

"Yeah, mate."

Lex yawned so wide her jaw cracked. "Is Wil here?" She asked.

"I don't know." If Wil wasn't there, the only thing Rhys could think to do was to send up metaphorical fire signals through the Plain Jane network. If anyone *could* help him, it'd be Wil's friends in the service industry. But *would* they? According to Wil, discretion was the name of their game.

He unbuckled his seatbelt and twisted in his seat to face first Lex, then Syd. "Wait here. I'm going to go see if anyone's awake." Or he would have if there wasn't a sharp rap at his window. "Hell!" Rhys jerked around, heart beating wildly. He twisted his key to flick on the car battery and pressed the control to slide his window down.

A statuesque man stood a few feet away. He looked like something out of a black and white movie—square jaw, dead straight eyebrows, silver hair...and Wil's dove grey eyes.

The man, who he could only assume was Wil's father, took a gander through Rhys' open window, his expression softening at the sight of the children. "Can I help? You look lost." At the sound of footsteps, Rhys looked over his shoulder to see another figure approaching, backlit by a window.

"Who is it, John?" A female voice.

Was it Wil's mother?

"A family. Don't worry, dear. I'll set their course to rights." Wil's father turned back to him. "Where are you headed, sir?"

Rhys waited to speak a beat too long, because Syd piped up from the back seat. "We're on a Wil hunt." And Lex asked, "Is he here?"

"Wil?" The bushy eyebrows went up at that. "Our Wil?"

No. My Wil.

But he couldn't say that. Instead, Rhys pushed open the car door and stepped out into the chill wind. Hand out-thrust, he shook the man's paper-dry hand. "I'm Rhys Buckley. Wil is...*was* my butler."

"Ah." Mr Haines' posture went taut as a bow-string, and he pulled his hand from Rhys' grip. "I see."

Far from discouraged, Rhys took the man's frosty reception as a win. It meant Wil had at least spoken to his parents. Even if it was only to complain about his boss' douchebaggery. It meant Wil might even be there—somewhere within the grandiose walls of Mistlethwaite Manor. Rhys pushed his wind-whipped hair out of his eyes and scanned the many dark windows. No sign. Not even a fluttering curtain. "I need to speak to him. To tell him..." He stopped himself. What he had to say was for Wil alone to hear. He returned to face Wil's father. "Please."

Mr Haines' mouth tightened.

"Please," Rhys repeated.

"Bring them inside, John." The woman stepped closer. Her voice was no nonsense. "Those poor children must be frozen to the bone."

"Thank you," Rhys said. No thought for how cold and weary he must be, but he supposed he probably deserved the snub. "Lex. Syd. Grab your things." He heard the rustling of jackets and their weekend backpacks, then the soft clunk of the passenger doors opening and closing as he scrolled up his window, grabbed his phone and charge cord from the central console, and flicked off the internal light, plunging them all into darkness.

The sound of the Range Rover's electronic locks pierced the night, and the orange indicator lights briefly illuminated the woman with her arm outstretched. "Come along. I'm sure I can rustle up some hot cocoa. Do you like marshmallows?"

Syd was off like a shot, around the corner, and down a half-flight of stairs to what looked to be the servant's entrance. Rhys hustled after Syd, uncomfortable not being able to see the boy in a strange place.

Mrs Haines led them down a short corridor to an enormous flag-stoned kitchen. "Wow." The space was cinematic in scale.

Mrs Haines sat Syd and Lex at a wooden table that was easily four times the size of their kitchen island back home. On the far wall, a six-foot-wide hearth, crowned by a hammered copper hood, sat beside an ancient black Aga, and *that* cozied up beside a run of modern stainless-steel ovens and cooktops. The contrast was surreal.

This was where Wil had grown up?

Rhys couldn't fathom it.

"Tea, Mr Buckley?" Mrs Haines asked.

"Thank you. Yes. I'd appreciate it." He'd suffer tea if it'd get him closer to fulfilling his goal. "I'd like to speak to Wil, if I could. He left without…" he'd been about to say 'he left without notice,' but that was an unfair attribution of blame. "Wil left before I could properly correct a misunderstanding." *Better, Rhys.* "Is he here?"

She nodded. "He is."

Oh, thank God.

Mr Haines stood to one side. "I don't think we should let—"

"Hush, John. It's not your decision to make," Mrs Haines admonished her husband, then directed a fierce glare at Rhys. "I don't like to see my son hurting."

"Nor do I." That was the absolute truth.

Her eyebrow went up, and it was so like Wil's that he almost laughed, but Mrs Haines was all seriousness. "I believe you have some grovelling to do."

"I do." That truth was also absolute.

"What does gruvering mean?" Syd asked around a mouthful of pink marshmallow.

"It means to ask for forgiveness," Rhys answered.

"Not exactly." Mrs Haines stirred the teapot three times, secured the lid, then slipped a knitted pot warmer over the top. "More accurately, it means to go down on one's proverbial knees and beg for forgiveness."

"Can't argue with that." He'd go down on his knees for Wil any day.

Mrs Haines held his gaze for an uncomfortably long time. Eventually, though, she spoke. "He seems earnest to me, John."

Rhys couldn't stop a relieved chuckle from bursting forth. "Wil gets his straight talk from the cradle, I see."

"More like from the womb," she winked. "Now, if it's alright with you, Mr Buckley, as soon as these two little crumpets have finished their cocoa, I'll take them through to our quarters. We have a sectional sofa where they can stretch out and get some rest."

"That's very kind. Thank you."

"Meanwhile, John will find you an extra jacket to wear."

"Why?" Were they housing his niece and nephew, while shoving him out into the cold and the dark?

She pointed to the ceiling. "Take him to the north tower, John. It's a bit nippy this late at night, and my guess is you'll be up there for a while."

Chapter 26

Wil

Wil wrote off the first screech of metal on metal. The higgledy-piggledy roofline of Mistlethwaite Manor had so many odd joins and angles it was a wonder the whole place didn't play a symphony when the wind was up. He tugged at the ropes on his hoodie till the only parts of him exposed were his eyes and the tip of his frozen nose, then snuggled down deeper into his nest of soft blankets.

Not sure if he wanted his mind free or full, Wil eyeballed the gap-toothed edging of the crenulated wall and traced the line between stone-cold black and starry, starry night. The Mistlethwaite estate wasn't all that far from the Dark Skies Reserve over Exmore National Park, where the lack of light pollution meant the heavens were so bright that the stars and planets and gaseous nebulas looked close enough to touch. Sleeping up there, under the stars, had never failed to raise Wil's spirits, until he'd lost both his job and the man he loved, all in one day.

High five, Wil. Excellent work.

Trouble was, it wasn't working so well. The roof had lost its magic. The starry night wasn't providing the helpful perspective he sorely needed. It wasn't his place of safety anymore. It wasn't home.

The sound came again, followed by a deep grunt, followed by shuffling footsteps and a wild slash of torchlight that sliced through the darkness.

Wil shut his eyes tight. Night-blindness was a pain in the arse.

"I don't need more tea, Dad," he yelled through the wind. He'd already drunk his way through one thermos, any more and he'd be racing for the bathroom. And *that* would put a serious crimp in his wallow session.

"M'not your dad."

Wil jerked his head up so fast he practically gave himself whiplash. "Rhys?"

"Hi."

"Holy fuck." *Are you real?*

"Ha! Wil Haines knows how to curse...the world must have shifted on its axis."

"What the hell are you doing here?" As Wil sat up, his hoodie slipped down, the chill barrelled in, and he hit the back of his head against the rough stone crenulation. "Ow, fuck!" *Jesus.*

The torchlight went haywire as Rhys ran forward and dropped to his knees on Wil's blankets, the wind stealing the fog of his panicked breath. "Are you alright?"

"Yes." *No. I'm moping on a rooftop. Of course, I'm not fucking alright.* His heart beat triple-time. "What cockamamy plan brought you all the way here?"

"I could ask you the same thing."

That didn't warrant an answer. He had every reason to run for the hills. "Seriously, Rhys. What are you doing here? I messaged my resignation. That's all there is to it. End of story."

"No, not the end." As Rhys crowded closer, the torchlight caught the side of his temple like the sliver of a crescent moon. "I came for you..."

Wil's heart lifted.

·   *Stupid heart.*

"To apologise. And to ask you..." Rhys' hands were ice cold, cupped around Wil's jaw.

Wil wanted to jerk away, but his traitorous body wouldn't let him.

Stupid body.

"Wil. Will you..." Rhys' voice broke, trembling with the shivers that wracked his body.

Wil couldn't stand it. He drew Rhys' hands down into the many layers of blankets that clumped in his lap when he sat up. "What is it? What's wrong?" Even after all that had happened, Wil couldn't stop his soul's instinct to care.

Stupid soul.

"Have me," Rhys said.

"Have you?" Was Rhys serious? Had he driven all the way to Devon for a shag on a rooftop? Unbelievable. "Now?"

"Always," Rhys said. He looked so earnest. Or perhaps that was a trick of the moonlight.

Could Wil have misunderstood? He took a deep breath, trying to slow his racing heart. "You want me here?" he asked, needing clarification. "On the roof? Under the stars? In the cold?" Nervous laughter welled like a swarm of fireflies in Wil's belly.

"Anywhere" Rhys said.

"Nuh-uh." That wasn't happening.

"I love you."

"You love me?" Wil echoed, disbelieving. Surely, he'd heard wrong.

"Yes."

Yes.

That one word hung in the air. Swirled with the wind. Spiralled across the galaxy.

"Wil, I don't want you to be some guy on the sidelines of my life, wearing white gloves and a diplomatic smile. I want to squabble with you about ridiculous things like etiquette and table place measurements and the correct way to issue invitations to a thousand more dinner parties. I want to have babies with your DNA, who cry politely and tell me I'm a crappy dad in the most civil, gracious way possible. I want to travel the world with you. I want to give you a free pass to my treehouse and a hand in my creations. But, most of all, I want you to claim me, Wil, and never let me go."

Wil heard the words, but surely that was the wind and his wishes coalescing into fantasy. "Why do all the crazy things happen to us when we're trapped outside in the cold and can't escape each other?"

That made Rhys frown. "Do you truly want to escape? I won't press you. Not if you don't feel for me the same way I feel for you." He pulled back an inch. "Do you want me to leave?"

Wil couldn't see Rhys' expression clearly. The moonlight barely leant him a sheen of silver. But he didn't need to see the man to remember all their moments together. Including the moments when he'd held back...the moments when he'd not let himself dream.

Time to be brave, Wil. Time to be true.

"No," he said, his voice barely louder than the wind. Wil cleared his throat and tried again. "No, I don't. Not if I'm honest. Not really. Not even a little bit. Not at all."

Rhys bit his lip—the flash of his teeth like starlight. "Does that mean...?"

"Yes. That means yes."

"Yes!"

"But only if you promise—"

"Anything."

Wil couldn't contain his grin. "To never make me watch *Cave in My Heart* ever again."

"Deal." Rhys planted a kiss on Wil's chapped lips. Clinging there. "Deal," he repeated, softer. Almost inaudible.

"Come here. Come see the stars with me." Wil lifted the covers, the bracing cold turning him into one giant shiver within half a second.

Rhys dove in. "Is that a euphemism for sex? Because, I don't think I can do it. I want you. Desperately. But my balls are already blue. They're likely to freeze off if we stay up here much longer."

"Shh." Wil wrapped his right arm tight around Rhys' shoulders and drew him close to his side. "We're not up here for that."

"Oh?"

Wil couldn't help but grin at the disappointment in Rhys' voice.

"Why did you come up here, then?" Rhys asked.

"To shed my cares into the night."

"Your cares, huh? Did it work?"

"Yeah." Wil rubbed his chapped lips against Rhys' beard, sending a hundred happy zings to his heart. "Seems that way."

Chapter 27

Rhys

R hys blindly searched for access to Wil's core. Despite the self-declared threat to his balls, nothing was going to stop him from touching Wil. Well...nothing except the multitude of layers between them.

"What are you doing?" Wil asked, as though it wasn't obvious.

"I'm on a quest." Rhys burrowed down through feather-down and fleece till all he could feel was a thin sheath of cotton covering Wil's chest. He flattened his hand and threaded his fingers along the grooves of Wil's ribs. The man was too slender. Clearly, Wil needed someone to feed him...to take proper care of him...to truly pay attention to his needs.

"For me?"

Hell, yes. "No." Rhys deadpanned. "To catalogue the abundant textiles on offer in the homeware store you must have raided before coming up here."

"You can thank my mother for that." Wil's chuckle was lost on a rush of breath as Rhys slid his thumb through the sliver of a gap between buttonholes. Teasing. And Wil arched up into his touch.

Something told Rhys it wasn't from ticklishness. "Please don't bring up your mother." Rhys flicked one shirt button out of its hole. Then another.

"Oh?" Wil grabbed for his wrist, but didn't stop Rhys in his mission. "Is this a no-parents-allowed quest?"

"Yep. That's exactly what it is. No parents." Rhys flicked open a third button and dipped his pinkie tip inside Wil's navel. What he wouldn't give to go deeper. "No children." Guided by Wil's treasure trail, he traced slowly south, the curls springy under Rhys' touch. "No friends." Wil's abs tightened in response. Encouraged, Rhys continued till his knuckles brushed the unwelcome resistance of Wil's belt buckle. "No foes," he added, wishing they were already naked, tussling in a warm bed. "Nobody but you and—"

"Us." A glint of starlight flickered in Wil's eyes.

Us. Rhys would have confirmed it, except Wil's grip on his wrist tightened, wrenched his arm out of the many layers, and rolled him over onto his back. "Mmm." Rhys moaned in happy surprise. *There's my fierce spitfire of a butler.*

Wil hovered over him, a rich shadow between Rhys and the heavens. And then the starlight was gone and Wil's lips were on his. An innocent closed-mouth kiss. Or, it would have been if Wil hadn't pressed his heat into the groove at Rhys' hip.

They groaned in unison.

"Want you." Rhys gripped the back of Wil's neck with his free hand, lifted into the kiss, and slanted to deepen the connection.

He nipped and tugged and laved at Wil's chapped lips, warming them, moulding them to meet his desire. Begging for entry.

Wil didn't disappoint. He opened to caress the sensitive inside of Rhys' lip with the dextrous tip of his tongue, claiming territory Rhys was more than happy to give up.

Rhys went seeking, too. Tasting. Touching. Drawing Wil in further. Loving the rasp of tongue against tongue. The sound of Wil's restrained moans. The desperate rush of blood in his ears and...elsewhere.

He twisted his hips, craving pressure. Needing relief.

"Wait," Wil abruptly let go of his wrist, and the heat at his hip disappeared.

Rhys stilled. Had he read things wrong? Had he pushed too far? Had he gotten so caught up in his selfish desire that he'd missed Wil's cues? He mentally rewound the night's events. If only he could see Wil's full expression—read his mind. "God, Wil. I'm sorry. We can wait." Waiting was the last thing Rhys wanted to do, but if Wil needed time to adjust to their new reality, he'd deal with it. Patience was a virtue. Right?

He could be virtuous.

Maybe.

The second he softened his hold on the back of Wil's neck, the muscles there bunched and flexed, but Wil said nothing. It was as if time stretched. Held taught like an elastic band. And then Rhys felt it.

Wil's hand.

On him.

Claiming Rhys for his own.

"What?" It was a stupid question to ask. The 'what' filled Wil's palm, trapped inside Rhys too-tight jeans. He humped up into the press of Wil's hand. Wanting more. Wanting everything. "Wil," he begged. "Don't tease."

Show me you want me as much as I want you.

Key-by-key, Wil slowly teased Rhys' jeans zipper down, and, like a puppet on a string, Rhys rose to Wil's silent command. Not that he needed much encouragement. If Rhys' body could speak, it would have delivered a treatise on desire.

Wil's hand slid inside his boxer briefs and gripped him tight.

The breath left Rhys body before he could even properly suck it in. So much for attending to Wil's needs. How had the tables turned so quickly?

He humped into Wil's dry grip. Who cared if he wound up with friction burns? Not him.

One thing was for sure—his balls weren't blue anymore.

Then came a wet kiss to the sensitive side of his neck. "Do you want this?" Wil asked, hot in his ear.

"Yes." Always, yes. Why would Wil even ask?

Wil's hand pulsed in a heady rhythm. It reminded Rhys of old Hollywood movies featuring synchronised swimmers—the throbbing ring of the water ballet. He didn't even need to imagine a soundtrack, the freezing wind took care of that, whistling around the crenulations and smoke-stacks, stealing his cry as he reached his peak and tumbled over into sweet oblivion.

Chapter 28

Rhys

In an effort to distract himself while Wil showered without him, Rhys had been trawling through the treasures on the bookcase in Wil's childhood bedroom when the bathroom door opened and Wil came out with a pink floral towel wrapped around his hips, shiny water droplets clinging to the light fuzz across his chest, and a billow of steam trailing behind.

The pattern on the towel messed with the porn vibe, but Rhys could look past it.

"Your turn," Wil said.

Rhys blindly replaced Wil's brass House Prefect pin back where he'd found it, then reached for the towelling knot at Wil's hip. His turn to give Wil the most satisfying orgasm of his life? "Hell, yeah."

"Behave." Wil skipped away, keeping the monastic distance he'd enforced ever since they'd stepped back under Mistlethwaite Manor's roof. "I meant it's your turn to shower."

Rhys tsked. "You're no fun."

"No. What's *not* fun is my mother hearing us together." It was abundantly clear what Wil meant by 'together', and how ghastly a prospect he thought that was.

Rhys got it. He did. No guy wanted his parents to hear him getting frisky. But surely, they were distant enough. Mistlethwaite Manor was mammoth. Rhys eyed the ugly damask wallpaper. "Aren't the walls in this palace, like, two-foot-thick?"

"It's a manor house, not a palace. And, yes, the outer walls would stand up to a battering ram. But the inner walls are lath and plaster. They're thin, and sounds carries when you have high ceilings." At that moment, a clang echoed from somewhere unknown. "See?" Pink-cheeked, Wil pulled open his heavy oak free-standing closet and took out boxer briefs and blue jeans, ironed to a crisp. He did an impressive switcheroo for the towel, giving Rhys far too little of a glimpse of the goods, then pulled out a teal merino crew-neck. Wil unfolded it and shrugged it on, arms first. When his head popped out, his wet locks flopped in his adorable face.

Unable to resist touching, Rhys stepped up close and finger-combed the dark blonde locks up into a messy version of Wil's usual neat quiff. "I like this look."

"What? A mess?" Wil's nostrils flared, and he tilted his head at Rhys' continued ministrations.

"Rumpled. Like we just got out of bed."

Wil's eyes skittered across to the single bed on the other side of the room, its covers still virginal. What Rhys wouldn't give to ruffle those up.

"How long do we have to stay in Devon?" Rhys asked. He probably ought to want to spend some time with Wil's family—to win their official approval—but he was too impatient for that, and the pink in Wil's cheeks told him he wasn't alone.

"Not long." Avoiding Rhys' gaze, Wil reached into the closet again and pulled out a black and red football jersey and dark grey jeans. "Here. They might be a bit snug, but they'll do. You go shower. I'll be back in a bit." He was already halfway to the door before Rhys could blink.

"Where are you going?"

"To bring down the blanket fort we left on the roof."

"And then?"

Wil twisted the doorknob. "Then, we do the walk of shame."

Shame? The only shame Rhys felt was for how bloody long it'd taken him to get his head on straight and realise how deeply he cared. None of that was on Wil. "It can't be that bad."

Wil thunked his forehead against the solid wooden door. "You don't know my mother. The butler hooking up with the boss? It's sacrilegious."

"I don't know. She seemed pretty cool when I met her. Protective, but cool. And we're not hooking up. This is not me asking you to add 'lover' to your resume."

"A good thing, since butler-lover isn't a thing." Wil said, as droll as droll could be. It made Rhys grin.

"My point is, there's nothing smarmy about this. About what's between us."

Wil rolled till his back was flat against the door, his head tilted back. He didn't make eye contact. "I know that. And you know that. But my folks are old school."

Old school.

What had Jacob said? Something about the upstairs-down-stairs divide. About tradition. About the pressure Rhys had inadvertently put on Wil to choose between their profession-al and personal relationships. It was a distinction Rhys rarely made. For him, professional *was* personal. His films wouldn't get made if he tried to keep an impersonal distance. But he and Wil weren't of the same ilk. For Wil, choosing one meant sacrificing the other—a sacrifice Rhys would never forget. Did Wil also feel like he had to give up his family for them to be together? Rhys would never do that. Family was sacred. "Hey." He moved close and hooked a finger through one of Wil's belt loops. "When I say I'm with you, I mean all of you. Not just the efficient butler with the hyper-optimized to-do list."

"No?"

"No. Sometimes the joy is in the mess." At Wil's frown, Rhys pressed a kiss to one corner of his mouth. "The preciousness."

"M'not precious."

Rhys drifted across and pressed a kiss to the other corner. "The awkwardness."

"Hmph." His lips twitched, unamused.

Rhys rubbed his beard against Wil's neat scruff. "The clum-siness."

"Hey!" Wil protested, but it was half-hearted. Facts were facts.

Rhys kissed the delicate skin at Wil's temple. "The weird-ness."

"Oh, now. That's you. Not me."

Rhys pulled back to see Wil's expression. "Not anymore, Wil. What's mine is yours, and what's yours is mine. Including—"

"My parents?" Wil proposed, getting back to the issue at hand. He looked zero kinds of sure about that prospect.

"For better or worse." Rhys pushed a rogue lock back off of Wil's forehead. "And there's not a single thing shameful about it."

Wil gave a tiny twist of a smile that had Rhys' heart pitter-pattering a mile a minute.

"Okay?" Rhys asked.

It took too long, but, finally, Wil answered, "Okay."

Never had such an innocuous word held so much promise. "Okay," Rhys repeated. "You go do your thing. I'll go shower. Then we face the music. And then—"

"We go home," said Wil.

Home. How sweet that sounded.

Not one to contain his pleasure, Rhys planted a kiss on Wil worthy of the ages.

"Go," he eventually said, adjusting himself as he stepped back to allow Wil to escape. And as he lathered up with Wil's silky goat's milk body wash, nothing could stop his imagination from tripping over thoughts of his butler, naked, in his arms.

Forever.

Fifteen minutes later, he and Wil entered the expansive kitchen to a wave of warmth and the most heavenly aroma. His stomach gurgled with hunger, and Wil's laugh was like champagne fizz in his heart. "Hush, you," he whispered into

Wil's ear. "It's your fault I haven't eaten in God knows how long."

Something must have alerted Mrs Haines to their presence. "Ah, there you are."

Mr Haines put his cup of tea down with a clatter, while Lex and Syd cried out in concert, "Wil!"

Lex came at him, pushing Rhys away to take Wil in a strangling bear hug.

"We went on a Wil-hunt." Syd's grin stretched wide across his face. "And we found you!"

"A Wil-hunt, eh?" Wil gave Rhys a side-eye, which he studiously ignored in favour of the goings on in the kitchen.

"What are you up to Syd?" His nephew was wearing a blue and white striped, flour-streaked apron, the waist tie hitched high under his armpits. "Looks like a blizzard swept through here." The table in front of his Syd was covered in drifts of flour, a giant mound of dough in the centre, and his hands were so white it looked like he was wearing Wil's silver-service white cotton gloves.

"It's flour. Not snow." Syd, ever the arbiter of truth, corrected him. "We're baking scones for a cream tea."

"That's the way, Sydney." Mrs Haines nodded. "Now, roll it out, just as your sister did." She handed Syd a wooden rolling pin as thick as his arm, and he beamed at the woman's open-hearted approval.

In an instant, Rhys saw a new vision of the future. A vision of family—of deep connection. And to think that he had Wil to thank for it. Wil, who'd come to Buck House with nothing but a suitcase and ambition. He'd not been a will-o'-the-wisp—there one minute, gone the next. No. His Wil had stayed. Or, he would have, if Rhys hadn't screwed up.

"Mum. Dad. This is Rhys. My, um..."

"Intended." Rhys knew when to hold back, and when it was best to declare himself.

"You're engaged?" Mrs Haines' voice rose alarmingly.

"No." Wil twisted to give him a glare. "He just means that we're together. That's all, Mum. Just...together."

Together? Yes. Just? There was nothing 'just' about how Rhys felt. *Why so hesitant?* He wanted to ask. But he knew why. Trust wasn't won overnight. He'd have to provide a lot of proof to make Wil believe, with bone-deep certainty, that Rhys was in it for real. For the long haul.

"Well, now..." Belatedly, Mr Haines came to his feet, too. He smoothed the front of his three-piece suit and tweaked the sprig of rosemary lodged in his lapel. "That's quite something, son."

"It is."

"Are you sure?" Mrs Haines asked.

"I'm surely sure." Wil's hand slipped into his, and Rhys gave it an affirming squeeze.

So, so sure.

"Surely, surely, surely sure..." Syd sung as he pressed a cookie cutter into the dough and placed the rounds on a buttered and floured baking tray, arranged in exacting rows a perfect thumb-length apart.

Meanwhile, one of the many ovens buzzed, and Lex leaped into action. "My scones!"

"Careful, Alexandra. It's hot. Mind you wear the mitts." Mrs Haines switched her ready attention to Lex, who swelled at the attention, just as Syd had. Under her direction, Lex pulled a tray of puffy, golden scones from the oven and tipped them straight into a cloth-lined basket. "That's the way."

Rhys' stomach gurgled again.

"Can we eat them straight away?" Lex asked, a sentiment Rhys concurred with, one-hundred percent.

"Almost. Let them steam off a tad first. If they're too hot, they'll burn your tongue."

Mr Haines gave the pot he'd been drinking from a testing swill. "You two will be wanting a cup of tea, I'm sure. There's plenty here."

"Tosh, John. Don't offer them that. It must be thick as Marmite by now. I'll make a fresh pot." She filled the kettle and placed it on the Aga hob.

The action was so familiar, it melted the last of Rhys' apprehension at facing Wil's parents. "I'm sure it's fine," he said. "Please don't go to any trouble for me." They'd already taken care of Syd and Lex through the night and half the morning, the last thing he wanted to do was take advantage of their welcome.

With a wicked glint in his eye, Mr Haines took a sip from his porcelain cup. "Puts hairs on your chest," he said, practically daring Rhys to try it.

"Even better." Rhys gave an exaggerated eyebrow waggle and side-eyed Wil. "I'm rather partial to hairy chests."

The tip of Wil's ear flamed, but Mr Haines didn't bat an eyelid, and Mrs Haines snorted. "You'll do, Rhys Buckley," she said.

Beaming, Rhys gave Wil's hand a last squeeze, then let go. He went to the impressive glass-fronted cupboards filled with crockery and searched for the classic floral Portmeirion cups and saucers that matched the teacup in Mr Haines' hand. He returned with two sets to the table and held one cup out for the man to fill, and gawd, yes, the tea looked like it had been steeping for an age. Gamely, Rhys took a sip, grimacing at the brackish flavour.

Mr Haines laughed. "Would you find the milk and sugar for our esteemed guest, son? I think he needs a little sweetening."

"Not really," he heard Wil mutter.

"And grab the clotted cream and blackberry jam while you're there, Wil. They ought to be on the top shelf of the refrigerator," Mrs Haines added as she helped Syd slide his tray of unbaked scone dough into the oven.

The kettle whistle went off, a new pot of tea was covered with a tea cosy that looked like a cabbage, and they all sat around the clean end of the table to enjoy the most scrumptious cream tea he'd ever had. "Oh my, God, Lex. They taste amazing. Here, Wil. Try this." He went to feed Wil a morsel of scone, loaded with jam and a dollop of rich clotted cream, but Wil pulled back.

"You did it wrong."

"Wrong?" Rhys frowned.

"That's the Cornish way. In Devon, the cream goes first, not the jam. Here." Wil held out a similar morsel for him, only dark blackberry jam dripped over the cream and down onto Wil's fingers.

Rhys shrugged. He didn't give two hoots what order the toppings went on. "As you wish." He opened wide and watched Wil's mouth mimicking his as Rhys took the treat in and licked the lingering sweetness from Wil's thumb. "Mmm," he hummed. "Perfect."

Chapter 29

Wil

S hortly after the oven buzzed for the second time, they
said their goodbyes.

"Are you sure you can't stay?" Mum asked as she wrapped
Syd's hot scones in a spare basket for them to take home to
Oxfordshire. "David and Marcia are coming up for after-
noon tea. It'd be lovely to have my boys back together."

"Not this time, sorry Mum. I'll wave to them on the way
out, but we've got places to be and a baby to see." Wil
shrugged on his jacket and collected his keys from the row
of hooks beside the kitchen's outer door.

Beside him, Rhys helped Syd with his coat. "Marcia?"

"The boys' nanny," Mum said, as though he and David
were both still six years old.

"David's *former* nanny, now his business partner. I think
I told you about her."

"The one with the impressive DVD collection?"

"That's the one."

Mum handed Syd the scones and smoothed back Lex's hair. "She and David run a nanny agency out of the gate house."

"Mannies, actually. *Mistlethwaite Mannies.*"

Rhys mouthed the words and grinned. "Cool." But when Wil jangled his car keys, Rhys' expression darkened. "Any chance you'd agree to leave your car here?"

"You don't like my rust bucket?"

"I like your rust bucket just fine. It brought you to me. But, today, I want to be together. You. Me. Us," he said, including the kids.

That sounded mighty fine, but... "How am I supposed to get around without it?"

"Buckle Up Productions can buy you a new car. As the CHO, you'll need something better for company business, anyway."

"CHO?"

"Chief Home Officer."

Chief Home Officer. It was Wil's turn to mouth Rhys' words. It'd take some getting used to, but he liked it. He liked it just fine.

"No offense, Mr Haines," Rhys said to Dad. "But I reckon it's an upgrade from butler."

"More of a lateral move, I'm inclined to think." Dad rocked back on his heels, pleased as punch by his pithy answer.

Wil could only roll his eyes at how successfully Rhys had charmed his folks.

There was a minor problem, though. "What about when you're away filming? I can't be CHO of Buck House *and* help you on location. According to Jacob, you're even more in need of a butler then."

"True." Rhys wrapped his arm around Lex's shoulders. "I'm hopeless when I'm away from Buck House. But I think that's all about to change."

"Oh, yeah?"

"Yeah. You'll be the CHO of me, not of Buck House. If I have you with me, I'll be home no matter where we go."

Mum practically melted, which was so very weird. Where had her precious dignity gone? The same way his had gone? Lapsed under the sway of Rhys Buckley's unique charm? Of his utter conviction that the value of an individual transcended social strata—that no one person mattered more or less than the next. In fact, if he asked him, Rhys would probably say that Wil was the boss of him, rather than the other way around.

Wil wasn't about to disabuse him of the notion.

With a bemused shake of his head at the surprise tangent his life had taken, Wil detached his car key from the ring holding his Buck House keys and hung it back on the hook. "As you wish," he said, and right there, in front of everyone he held dear, Wil went up on his toes and pressed a soft kiss to Rhys' jam-sweet lips.

The road was a blur of motorway signs and pit stops and "yellow car!" calls from the back seat, and they made it back to Reading in time to dash into the labour ward to see Evangeline and baby Poppy before the midwives hustled them out at the end of visiting hours. The most direct route back to the Maxwell School conveniently took them past The Lion and Lamb, where they occupied their favourite booth for an early supper. Soon Lex and Syd were gone with waves from him, air kisses from Rhys, and embarrassed groans from the kids. And then, as dusk descended over Hewstoke Woods, Rhys steered the Range Rover down through the high green hedge groves, swept over the clanking wooden bridge, turned off onto leaf-strewn Oak Tree Lane, and pulled up in front of the black ironwork gate to Buck House.

The car had a button Rhys could use for automatic entry, but he didn't use it. Instead, he rolled down his window to press the red teardrop doorknob and pointed at the four familiar options that lit up the touchscreen on the gothic dollhouse.

What is the nature of your visit?

1: Family

2: Business

3: Mischief

4: Lost

"What's your answer?" Rhys asked.

Wil couldn't help but recall the first day he'd arrived at the gate. The same, but so, very different. "Not business."

"Not today," Rhys agreed.

"And I'm definitely not lost."

"Hell, no."

"Hmm..." Wil hummed, pretending to ponder. "I probably should say family."

The lights of the dash lit up Rhys' grin, telling Wil they had a very similar idea in mind.

"But, tonight, I'm thinking...maybe...I've come for a spot of mischief."

"Hell, yeah." The engine revved, the gate swung open, and finally, they were home. "Come on." Rhys didn't even let him get one leg out of the car before he was tugging at Wil's hand.

"Where are we going?"

"You'll see." Instead of going through the front door, Rhys led him around the side of Buck House, past the windows to the sitting room and dining room, past the kitchen door, and around to the back to the base of Rhys' tree. There, he stopped and rang the bell.

Was Rhys nervous? Why?

Wil looked up. Was Rhys planning to welcome him into his treehouse? His inner sanctum? His space of grace? For some reason, the thought felt more personal than anything else. More personal even than physical touch. Because Rhys was all about his inner world—his imagination—a place nobody could go but him. "Are you sure?" Wil asked, his heart tripping with his own nerves. The treehouse was the final hurdle. Once he went in, there'd be no going back.

"More than sure."

"Surely sure?"

In answer, Rhys put Wil's hand to the rung at chest height. He shone his phone light at the trapdoor on the base of the treehouse, and said, "Up you go. The padlock code is triple six."

That deserved an eye roll. "Of course, it is. You rebel, you."

It was dark inside. The three porthole windows on the outer walls were too small to let much of the twilight in. But as soon as Rhys' head popped through the hatch behind Wil, he must have flicked a switch somewhere because a dense twine of white fairy lights sparked from corner to corner to corner.

"Oh!"

Heaven.

The space was tiny, but tall enough for Rhys to stand, which meant he could, too.

Curious, Wil took the space in. One quarter of the tree-house was occupied by a built-in wooden desk, topped with a tech set up that rivalled his own office in the house. An ergonomic saddle seat was tucked underneath, and the telltale orange bars of a space heater warming up. And on the opposite side of the square treehouse was a nest of cushions atop a pile of yoga mats that must have been at least twenty layers thick.

Below the fairy lights, a shallow bookshelf ran at eye-height along all four walls. Below that ran a ribbon of laminated white paper, almost as narrow as old-fashioned film strip, divided up into dozens of rectangles filled with colourful stick figure cartoons in wacky poses in front of rudimentary backgrounds.

"Is that a storyboard for one of your movies?"

"Yep. My first."

Wil ran his eye along the length of it. "It doesn't look anything like *Saturnine.*"

"No, it's a horror short I made in film school. I'll show you sometime." Rhys came up close behind him, tugged his jacket off, and pressed a kiss to his neck. "Not tonight, though."

No. He shivered, but it wasn't at the sudden chill. The night ahead was for other things. Wicked things. "Are you sure me being here won't mess with your flow?"

Rhys cracked a laugh. "It's not my flow I want you to mess with tonight."

"Oh. Well, then..." Devoid of further objections, Wil let himself be drawn down to kneel beside Rhys onto the many-layered yoga mats.

"Well, then." Rhys' dark eyes glinted. He ghosted a kiss across Wil's lips. Far too soft to satisfy. "Alone at last."

At last. Wil shivered.

"It'll warm up soon enough. The space heater is pretty efficient."

"That's not what made me shiver."

"No?"

"No." Wil threaded his fingers through Rhys' and brought both hands around his waist, demonstrating with action what he couldn't bring himself to say in words.

Hold me. Take me. Make me yours.

"Are you sure?" Rhys asked. "I don't want you to think—"

Wil pressed a finger to Rhys' lips, then replaced it with his own, sipping at Rhys' warmth. A nudge, a nip, a flick of tongue was all it took to get Rhys on board. As if slow-dancing, he curled his arms around Rhys' neck and gave himself over. Not a single doubt in his heart.

"Wil." Rhys' hands firmed at the small of his back, pressing his urgent heat close, leaving nothing to the imagination. A deeper kiss. All caution gone. And then he was lowering Wil into the cosy nest of mats and cushio—

"Ouch!" Something hard was right under his tailbone. He arched away from it, up into Rhys, and they both groaned as they rolled sideways till Rhys was flat on the hard floor with Wil spread-eagled on top.

Breathless, Rhys asked, "You alright?"

"Yeah." He kept one hand protectively under Rhys' head and reached to feel through the cushions for the offending rock, or whatever the hell it was that'd caused the very unwelcome disruption.

"What is it?"

"Don't know. Something hard poked me in the arse."

Rhys snorted and his hands drifted lower down Wil's back. "Hate to break it to you, but that 'something hard' is my—"

"Don't say it." He nipped Rhys' lower lip. Not sharp enough to draw blood, but it did shut him up. "God. Can we not have one single moment of classy intimacy?" Wil huffed. He shoved his fingers between the layers, searching for whatever had attacked his tailbone.

Rhys's hands slid back up. "You want classy?" His voice was low.

Shit. "Sorry. I didn't mean that. I just want everything to be right. For this to be..." How could he explain the rush he got when everything was in alignment? Right place. Right time. Right everything.

Rhys's gaze dodged past him. "If you're looking for Champagne and roses, I'm afraid you've burrowed your way into the heart of the wrong man."

"No." Wil pressed his forehead to Rhys', caught the glint of fairy lights in his eyes, and held them firm. Unwavering. "No, Rhys. You are absolutely the right man for me. I wouldn't want this any other way. Except for the...ah-ha!" From what must have been the seventh or eighth layer—he'd lost count—Wil found the bastard thing and pulled it out.

"What is it?" Rhys asked, then laughed when Wil held it where they could both see. "An acorn? Jesus, Wil, it's like *Princess and the Pea*."

That deserved a glare. "I am *not* a princess. And this fucker is *not* the size of a pea."

Rhys snorted, which wasn't exactly the reaction Wil had been looking for, so he shoved his very much non-princess parts into Rhys' equally non-princess parts. Just to reinforce the point.

Rhys' head reared back, and he gripped Wil's hips so hard he'd probably leave fingerprint-sized bruises...right by the one the fucking acorn had surely given him.

Wil gasped, too late recognising that a little restraint might've been a good thing. "Oops."

"Oops?" Rhys panted. "Shit, Wil. I hereby give you permission to oops any time, day or night."

Wil didn't quite know what to say to that, so he reverted to his butler training, did exactly as he was bidden, and oopsed again...and again.

And again.

Hours later, sunrise flooded through the eastern porthole window and illuminated their cosy nest, turning Rhys' pale chest to rose gold and putting stars in Wil's eyes. Not that he needed them. Rhys provided all the star-power he'd ever need.

Loathe to move from his happy spot in the crook of Rhys' shoulder, Wil played with the acorn, idly thumbing the smooth and rough surfaces. Weird how things had turned out—how he'd gone looking for a working home, and found a loving one instead. Never in his wildest dreams had he expected that.

He felt Rhys thumb his bare shoulder, smooth as the acorn. "You should plant it," Rhys said.

"Yeah?" The idea appealed, but it was the seed of an oak tree. "They grow pretty slowly," he pointed out. They'd agreed they were in it for the long haul, and he believe Rhys. He did. But, still, Wil couldn't help pressing—to make sure all the 'i's were dotted, and all the 't's were crossed.

"Decades, I'd imagine," Rhys agreed, his expression free and easy. "Good thing you'll be around to watch it take root and grow."

Heart bursting at Rhys' clear certainty, Wil transferred his gaze back to the eastern window. The sun shone white gold by then, and dust motes danced light fireflies in the light. "Where would we sow it? In the garden?" A match for Rhys' grand oak? He didn't have Rhys' powerful imagination, but he could see their trees standing tall, side by side.

"No. Not in the garden," Rhys said. The too-easy exclusion caused Wil's heart to sink, but Rhys didn't seem to notice. "Oaks are majestic trees. We should plant it in the woods nearby—lend a little order to the wilderness."

His heart lifted. "Yeah?" He could do order.

"In the bluebell woods, perhaps," Rhys continued. "A tree fit for a prince, surrounded by a carpet fit for a king."

"Oh." How lovely that sounded. And, suddenly, Wil realised that Rhys wasn't just welcoming him into his heart and his home. He was welcoming Wil into his whole joyous, boundless, wonderous life.

Something of Wil's feelings must have been written on his face, because Rhys' intense eyes darkened, honing in on him. "I can't wait to show you the bluebells when they bloom. It's another world."

Wil rolled in and planted a simple kiss to Rhys' collarbone. "Don't need another world," he said. "I've got all I need. Right here. With you."

Thank You!

Thank you so much for reading *Where There's a Wil, There's a Way*!
If you enjoyed Wil and Rhys' story, and would like to help other readers find it, please consider leaving a rating or review!

For quirky content and updates on future books, subscribe to my newsletter at https://ptambler.com/newsletter-sign-up/

Also By PT Ambler

Tennyson Bend:

Haven

Deuce

Thrall

⸺ *ell* ⸺

Duly Domesticated

Where There's a Wil, There's a Way

I'll Make a Manny Out of You

⸺ *ell* ⸺

For an updated list, please visit:

ptambler.com/books

About PT Ambler

PT Ambler is an Aussie mm romance author who gets a ridiculous amount of joy letting her guys run rampant on the page.

Other fun things include sing-along road trips, zoning out in nature, day dreaming, people-watching in cafes, and coffee...smooth, delicious coffee, covered in shavings of rich, dark chocolate...mmm...

One of these days, she's going to write a novel set in a café about a gorgeous barista who... (PT drifts away into a caffeine-fuelled daydream).

To find out more, check out https://ptambler.com, sign up for my newsletter at https://ptambler.com/newsletter-sign-up /, or catch me (occasionally) on Instagram at https://www.ins tagram.com/pt_ambler/.